Her Rogue for One Night

Her Rogue for One Night

WICKED WIDOWS' LEAGUE
BOOK TWO

DAWN BROWER

"...when pain is over, the remembrance of it often becomes a pleasure."

— JANE AUSTEN, PERSUASION

Contents

EXCERPT: TO BARGAIN WITH A ROGUE

EXCERPT: A LADY NEVER TELLS

This is a work of fiction. Names, characters, places, and incidents are products of the author's imagination or are used fictitiously and are not to be construed as real. Any resemblance to actual locales, organizations, or persons, living or dead, is entirely coincidental.

Her Rogue for One Night © 2023 Dawn Brower

Cover art by Mandy Koehler Designs

For all those that find strength when they need it most. Do not give up. You never know what you might discover in the middle of your journey.

Prologue

Claudine Grant glanced up at the dark clouds in the sky. They were an omen of some sort. She had a feeling in her stomach that unsettled her and had since she'd woken earlier that morning. That feeling of dread wouldn't go away, and as the day progressed, it worsened.

Even if the clouds were not an omen of bad things to come, they alerted her to one thing with certainty. A storm was brewing. She should go back inside, but she couldn't make her legs move.

She had a letter from her husband, James, waiting for her inside. Claudine hadn't opened it yet. Letters from James rarely came. He was away at war fighting against Napoleon. It seemed like an endless war, and she feared she would never see him again. What if this was the last letter she ever received from him?

They married one day before he left for war. Their marriage had been quick. Well, as quick as it could be done. The banns were read and after the third week they said their vows. They'd had one night together, and then he had to leave. Then she was alone in their small home. Claudine had two servants—a maid and a cook. James was the third son of a viscount. His commission had given him his rank and position. He was a lieutenant in the Calvary.

All Claudine wanted was for her husband to return to her. She should read his letter. She glanced up at the sky once more and headed home. It didn't take her long to reach the entrance. She went inside and to her writing desk. Claudine pulled out the letter and broke the seal. Inside another letter had been folded inside. It only had her name scrawled across it. Her hands shook as she picked it up. It wasn't in James' handwriting. Who else would send her a letter?

She set it aside and ran her fingers over the

words James had written her. His handwriting was so familiar to her. She finished unfolding it and started to read it from the beginning.

My Dearest Claudine,

Today was a good day. There are not too many of those here. The sky was a brilliant blue, and the sun bathed us in its light. The warmth felt wonderful against my skin. I wish I could have enjoyed it more. I wish I could have spent this day with you cradled in my arms.

This letter I'm writing out of necessity. These words should come from me. If the worst should happen... God, I can't imagine the worst. Everyone should be able to live their lives with the freedom of not considering that possibility. As a soldier, I am not so fortunate. If I had not chosen this life, I would be with you.

But if that possibility should happen, I don't want to leave anything unsaid.

My wonderful, beautiful wife—I adore you. There are no words that can adequately describe how much I love you. The greatest day of my life was when you agreed to be my wife. Our wedding day will be forever honored in my memory. As far as regrets go, that is one thing that will not be tallied under that column. My heart will forever be yours. I will always belong to you, and only you.

My hope is that this letter will be fodder for a fire one day and you will never read it. That soon I'll be home and kissing you, loving you, and spending the rest of my days by your side. However, I must be pragmatic. If you are receiving this letter, then, my love, I am no longer amongst the living. Confirmation will come from someone of authority, but for now, this will have to do.

Before I left, I ensured that all my particulars were in order. You will be taken care of, and if you so choose, you *may remain in the home we lived in together. If it doesn't suit you, sell it and find another. And my love...try to let me go. I want you to be happy. Please visit my father. He will handle everything. I've already spoken to him about you and what should be done.*

All my love,
James

A tear fell down her cheek. She should have avoided reading the letter longer. She could have remained in blissful ignorance. This couldn't be real. James was not dead. Claudine refused to believe it. She picked up the other folded piece of paper. There was a quick note jotted down there. Almost as if an afterthought...

She needed to read the letter. Claudine's hands shook as she stared down at the parchment. The missive wasn't long. Perhaps that meant it wasn't the news she feared? No. That possibility was unlikely. She had to read it and find out. All the supposition was not helping her.

Dear. Mrs. Grant,

I served with Lieutenant James Grant. He is...was an honorable man. He died in service to his country. You can be proud of the man he was and all that he did. His actions saved the lives of several men in our unit. Without him, there would be more men being mourned. I am sincerely sorry for your loss. Lieutenant Grant will be missed by us all.

Yours truly,
Colonel Andrew Roberts

This letter sounded far more official. She should visit James' father right away. He should know more about what James' letter inferred to. She closed her eyes and held back the tears that threatened to fall. Now was not the time for giving in to tears. It was time to plan and get answers.

Claudine glanced out the window. The storm had rolled in. The sky had opened up and rain poured down. It bang against the window like a constant beat of a drum. The roads would be muddy in the morning, making them nearly impassible. She would not let that fact stop her. This trip was too important. She'd pack and go to London in the morning. There she would visit the viscount and find the truth. Whatever that truth might be...

One

Claudine didn't understand why she was about to visit the Dowager Countess of Wyndam. When she had received the invitation, she had considered declining it, but then reconsidered. She had been staying with her husband's father for several months, and she longed to return to her home in the country. There was no reason to stay in London any longer. In another few months she could go into half mourning or just skip that part if she so wished—did she really want to don clothing to announce to the world she was a widow? She had to move on with her life and try to let go of her husband once and for all.

She walked up to the townhouse. The door was a rich mahogany, but other than that, nothing stood out about the elegant home. It was simple, but Claudine would never live anywhere this nice. Not that there was anything particularly wrong with her home. It was enough and always had been. If her husband had lived through the war, they would have been blessed to have it to raise their family. She would probably never have a family—she couldn't imagine ever remarrying.

Claudine lifted the knocker and rapped it twice against the door and stood back to wait. Not long after that a gentleman with silver hair opened it. "Yes?" He lifted a brow.

"I have an appointment with Lady Wyndam," she told the man.

"Please come in," he said. "Do you have a card?"

She sighed. Claudine did not have any calling cards. There had been no reason to have any made. She did not pay calls on anyone and considered the expense too frivolous. "I do not..."

"It isn't necessary, Bracken." a woman said from behind the man. Her golden blond hair was twisted into a chignon and her blue eyes were sharp with hidden wit. "I'll escort Mrs. Grant to see the countess. She's expected."

Claudine frowned. How had this woman known who she was on sight? She had never met her before.

The blonde woman was quite pretty, but dressed in a no-nonsense dark blue dress. It was as plain as the woman was beautiful. It had no embellishments to even give the impression of trying to be attractive. Who was this woman?

"I am Miss Juliet Adams," the woman supplied in a quick introduction. "I am Lady Wyndam's paid companion, and I assist her with everything she may need." She gestured for Claudine to follow her. They stopped outside a room with a door closed. "Please wait here while I inquire if the countess is ready to receive you."

She didn't feel all that welcome. Was this how a servant felt? Were they required to languish in the hall until their betters could pay them any mind? Probably not... Likely they had more freedom to come and go than Claudine had.

Luckily, she didn't have to wait too long before Juliet returned. The woman smiled at her. There was something mischievous there, but Claudine couldn't pinpoint what. "Go through this door. Then there is another on the opposite side of the room. Knock twice and she'll let you know once you can enter. Good luck."

Why was she wishing her luck? What was this, and why did Lady Wyndam wish to see her? This was all rather confusing, and she didn't understand any of it. Perhaps once she met with the countess, all would make better sense. At least she hoped so... She followed Miss Adams' instructions and went through the door, then knocked on the next one. It didn't take long for her to get a reply.

"Come in, Mrs. Grant," a woman encouraged from the other side. "There's much we need to discuss."

She walked into the room and then over to an elderly woman. The countess had dark brown hair that was streaked with gray, and warm brown eyes. She fidgeted as she stood before the older woman. Should she say something? She didn't have any experience with these types of situations. The woman stared at her for several moments and then ordered, "Sit and tell me your story?"

"My story?" She nearly stuttered those two words out. "I don't understand." Claudine was even more confused than before, but she could do one thing. She sat down in a chair across from the woman and waited for her to respond.

"Tell me how you came to marry your lieutenant," Katherine told her. "Then we can move on from there."

She didn't talk about her husband with anyone.

No one ever asked her about him or their courtship and marriage. It was something she kept inside her head and revisited when the pain of losing him was especially difficult. Some days were worse than others. She was far too young to be a widow already. Though to be fair, she probably wouldn't have married James so soon if he wasn't about to leave for war. Their courtship had been fast and intense. She had loved him or believed she had. Either way, she had cared a great deal for him and was sad he'd died.

"James was a handsome man." She smiled as she tilted her head to the side. "He loved me so." Claudine twisted her fingers together. "I suppose I loved him too." She lifted her gaze to meet the countess's. "Is it wrong to question that now?"

"No dear," she said in a soft tone. "It means you understand yourself. In that, you're lucky. Not everyone as young as you are, do."

Lady Wyndam nodded at her. "Finish your story." Claudine began speaking again, and the countess leaned back to listen to her tale. It wasn't a very long one. It was simple enough. "We met at the country fair near my home. My father is a country squire. We were not poor, but nowhere near as wealthy as James's father. I had no dowry and nothing to offer, but he still wanted me. He married me without telling his family of his intentions." She closed her eyes and drew a deep breath. "I lived near the Scottish border, you see. It was easy enough to cross over and say our vows. Once that was done, no one could object, and trust me, many did. My father included..."

"What did your father have to say?" Lady Wyndam asked.

"He told me that I'd regret marrying James. He was the second son of a viscount—not the heir, but the family would always look down at me. My mother was Scottish and my father a mere squire. He could do far better than me as a bride." She glanced down at her hands and frowned. "Perhaps my father was correct, but he didn't live to see the outcome. He died a few months after James left for France."

"Did his family have issue with your marriage?" Lady Wyndam leaned forward on her ornate cane. It was mahogany, with a sapphire on the handle. "What happened next?"

"James has—had a cottage of his own. He purchased it after he bought his commission. He wanted a place of his own away from his family. It was still close enough to the viscount if he wished to visit, but far enough he had some freedom. He took me there after we married, but before he told his father of our marriage. I think he knew the viscount wouldn't welcome me outright."

"And was that the case?" The countess lifted a brow.

"Yes and no," Claudine said. "At first, both of his parents were livid..." She sighed. "After he left for France, they both visited me separately. I came to know them and...it was different. They were kinder to me and accepted I was a part of their family. I wrote to James and explained it all to him. He was happy they were being so courteous."

"But were you happy?"

"I had no reason not to be." Until he died... "Everything seemed perfect." But it hadn't been. In her heart, she couldn't help thinking she had made a mistake.

"Marriage is rarely that." Lady Wyndam smiled. "Even the most loving unions have strife from time to time. Husbands don't always tell their wives everything—even important details they should. My own husband was like that, and I loved him dearly. He made plans for my life that I wished he hadn't. Was that the case for you?"

Claudine nodded. "He did." She had been so

mad at James when she realized what he had done. He'd made plans for her life as if she were a child unable to make decisions for her own life.

"What did he do?" The countess asked in a kind tone.

"He made his father my guardian, should something happen to him. I've been living with the viscount ever since James' death. I'm under his protection until I remarry, and he has to approve that marriage."

"There is no other way for you to gain your freedom?" The countess frowned. "Do you even wish to remarry again?"

"If I do not remarry in five years, I can keep the home that James provided for me with a yearly allowance to do as I wish." She nibbled on her bottom lip. "I am trying to convince the viscount to allow me to return there until I am out of mourning. I'll go into half mourning in a few months."

"Will you now?" The countess's lips twitched as if she fought a smile. "Or are you doing that as an excuse to retire away from society?"

"I haven't decided," she told her. "What does society have to offer me?" She had never had a debut season and would never have one.

"Perhaps there is something I can offer you that

is far better than hiding for the rest of your life, or at least the next five years." The countess rapped her cane on the ground. "I have an offer for you that I do hope you will not refuse."

What could Lady Wyndam possibly have to offer her? She didn't need a companion. That was what Miss Adams was in the townhouse for. Unless she'd found a different position and Lady Wyndam hoped to replace her. She should quit trying to guess and just outright ask. "What is your proposal?"

"I, along with several friends, widows to be more precise, created a place that widows, young and old, could consider safe." She gripped her cane harder. "We all had experiences that clouded our lives after our husbands died and we wanted to help other widows in need."

"That sounds lovely." She still didn't know why Lady Wyndam had asked her there. "What does that have to do with me?"

"Isn't it obvious?" She quirked a brow upward. "I want you to join the league, and I hope that you will join our council. I think you're a suitable replacement for the widow that is no longer with us. We need to start adding some younger women that will be a part of the group for the future of the league."

"The league?" Claudine tilted her head to the side. "Do you have meetings?"

"Sometimes," Lady Wyndam said. "When it is needed and on a quarterly basis..." She sighed. "There are rules, of course, and I'll go over them all with you. But first I must ask if you're interested."

Was she? Claudine didn't have any friends, and she liked the idea of a group of women to spend time with. Especially if they were widows like herself. They would probably understand her more than most. "I am," she said firmly. "What do I need to do?"

"I'm so glad you asked." Lady Wyndam grinned. "I think we are going to be quite close the two of us. Let me order some tea and we will go over everything." She pointed to a nearby rope. "Be a dear and pull that for me. That will signal Juliet to bring in our refreshments."

Claudine stood and did as she asked, then returned to her seat. She couldn't wait to hear all the details. Perhaps there was more for her life than hiding in the country after all.

Two

One year later...

Claudine's scheduled time at Matron Manor had been up for a few days, but she didn't want to leave. Matron Manor had become her refuge. She preferred being at the estate for the Widows' League and actually disliked going to London at all. Lady Wyndam had insisted she return to London twice already, and she expected she would do the same soon. If she were not forced to leave, she'd gladly hide at Matron Manor.

The foyer was one of her favorite rooms at the manor. It had a grand staircase with a regal red carpet cascading down the steps. At the top of the first flight were portraits of the original five widows that had formed the league, with Lady Katherine Wyndam's in the center. Claudine admired all these women and the fortitude they must have had to create a safe place for any widow in need, and she was still baffled Lady Wyndam had chosen her to become a part of the Council of Five.

One of the founding widows passed away six months before Claudine had become a widow herself. They had left the position vacant all that time, but the other widows had been pressuring the council to fill her vacancy. The Council of Five was the governing body for the league of widows, and now she was the newest inductee.

Some widows that had been members far longer than her had been angry she'd been appointed. Claudine didn't understand that decision any more than they did. Lady Wyndam had said she reminded her of Mrs. Williamson, the founding widow that had died. Her coloring was similar to the lost widow, and she had been married to a lieutenant as well, but that was all she really knew about her. She had to take Lady Wyndam's word for it. Either way, she didn't regret her decision to join the league. She finally felt as if she found a place she belonged.

"Claudine," a woman said. "Do you have a moment?"

She turned toward the woman and pasted a smile on her face. Not that she wasn't glad to help, but she was sad she'd have to return to London soon. She took more rotations at Matron Manor than most because she enjoyed being there. "Yes, Eden?" Eden, or more accurately, to most of society, the Dowager Countess of Moreland, had golden blonde hair and light green eyes. She was truly lovely, and not more than a year or two older than Claudine. Eden was sad, but Claudine suspected it wasn't because of her husband's death. She hadn't said as much yet. They were becoming good friends, though, and she expected her new friend would confide in her soon.

"This is my first time being on rotation." She nibbled her bottom lip. "I am afraid I might mess up."

"Impossible," Claudine said in a reassuring tone. "We all do things differently. If you're ever uncertain, just refer to the guidebook. The rules are all there and any advice widows before us felt we might need to be successful in all our endeavors."

Eden's cheeks pinkened a little. "I have um..." She cleared her throat. "Read some of the more risqué entries in there." The dowager countess leaned in and said in a hushed tone, "Do you ever consider taking a lover?"

Claudine hadn't. Relations with her husband hadn't been unpleasant, but they also had been anything she liked enough to do it with a man outside of marriage. She'd heard that certain men make it far more pleasurable. Claudine had her doubts about the veracity of that rumor. She didn't quite know how to answer Eden, though. Claudine didn't wish to discourage her from any path she may be interested in. "Honestly," Claudine began. "I have been too busy to give it much thought." That wasn't a lie. She had been preoccupied. "Are you considering it?"

Eden shook her head. "No," she began. "I mean that is..." She sighed. "My husband's sister has her debut season soon. It made me wonder how I'd react if I am propositioned. It may happen once I am out in society with her. I'm a young widow and some scoundrel might think I'm ripe for the picking, so to speak."

Claudine laughed. "You're not wrong. Take some time to think about what you want. Once you know, then the answer will be obvious, and if you need to discern the best course of action after that, the guidebook has plenty of sage advice. Some of those widows even went on to marry again and find love. Is that something you're interested in?"

Eden closed her eyes and took a deep breath. When she opened them, there was resolve settled into her green eyes. "I never loved my husband. He was a reprobate and had an affair with my closest friend. That is what led to his death. I can't miss him." She shook her head vehemently. "Our marriage was arranged by our fathers. I don't regret it. I have a beautiful son from our union, but as to love..." She shrugged. "No, I am not against the possibility; however, I'm also not seeking it."

"Then there is your answer. Why plan our future when it's so freeing to have some choices with our lives? My husband thought to arrange my life even in death. His father has complete control over my funds. If not for the league, I'd be forced to live with him and ask him for everything. I won't be treated as if I'm a child without a mind of my own. I thank every day that Lady Wyndam invited me to join."

"Me as well." Eden grinned. "My benefactor was Lady Sylvan." She gestured toward the portrait of the fiery red-haired marchioness at the top of the staircase. "This was her home before the league was created. She donated so widows had a safe haven."

Claudine nodded. "She's quite outspoken too. There's nothing the marchioness is afraid to say. I admire that about her."

"She's my mother's godmother." Eden sighed. "When she heard about William's indiscretions and death, she said she regretted he died so quickly. She'd have liked to do the honor herself."

"You mentioned he had an affair with your friend," Claudine prompted. This was the most Eden had said to her before this moment. "Pardon me for asking...what happened?"

Eden groaned. "I'm surprised you didn't hear. It was all everyone talked about for a while..." She waved her hand dismissively. "It was a couple months after Christmastide. We had a house party. William and Claire—Lady Harewood, were having an affair during that time. Lord Harewood caught them and they fought. I don't think Lord Harewood meant to kill William, but that doesn't change the outcome."

How awful... "I'm sorry you had to go through all that." Claudine had lost her husband during the war. "How long ago was this?"

"A couple of years ago now," she said. "Long

enough for me to go through the expected mourning period and now Roslyn—my sister by marriage, to have her debut."

"I'm sure she'll be glad that you'll be at her side as she navigates the waters of society." Claudine's lips tilted upward. "I've never had a season of my own, and I don't particularly wish to become embroiled in it now."

"No?" Eden lifted a brow, then laughed. "Honestly, neither have I. Since my marriage was arranged, no one thought I should even bother with a debut season. I won't be much help to poor Roslyn, I'm afraid." She sighed. "I'll be as green as her. It's bound to be a disaster."

"Perhaps..." Claudine frowned. "But if you're truly worried, there has to be a widow or two that can help you. I'll ask Lady Wyndam, who she might believe will be of assistance. I wouldn't want you to go through it all blind—we both know society is filled with people that say one thing, then do the opposite." They would walk all over poor Eden... Claudine wouldn't fare any better in her place, either.

"I would appreciate that," Eden said earnestly. "Even if it is just offering a bit of advice. I fear I'll need all the help I can muster." She sighed again.

"Roslyn is also headstrong and will most likely be a difficult debutante. I wish someone else could be her chaperone."

"I don't envy you," Claudine told her. "But I'll support you with whatever I can." She took her role in the league seriously.

Eden didn't have time to respond before a maid walked over to them. "Pardon the interruption," the maid said. "But this arrived for you a little while ago." She handed a missive to Claudine, then curtsied and left them alone. Claudine sighed and tore it open quickly.

> My dearest Claudine,
>
> I expected your return days ago. If you're reading this, that means you didn't depart as expected. Don't make me send someone to fetch you. Come to London posthaste.
>
> Lady Wyndam.

She'd been expecting the summons. She should have just left Matron Manor when it was time.

"Is it bad news?" Eden asked.

Claudine shook her head. "Not at all. Lady

Wyndam is just reminding me I am expected in London. The council meets in a week and I must be there for it." At least it shouldn't take long to travel to London. Otherwise, Lady Wyndam would be even more disappointed in her. "I must go prepare to leave. She won't be pleased if I dally any longer than I already have." Claudine smiled at Eden. "If you need any more advice, you know where to find me. You'll do fine. Don't worry overmuch about something that hasn't even happened yet. Take one day at a time."

After departing that bit of wisdom, she left Eden alone. Eden had been in the league far longer than Claudine had, but this was her first time taking a rotation. She has a young son and hadn't wanted to be parted from him. He was spending some time with her parents for a couple of weeks and had volunteered to finally take time at Matron Manor.

Claudine hadn't been burdened with Children from her marriage. If she had loved James as much as she thought she had, it might have bothered her more not to have a child to remember him easier. Now she was grateful she hadn't been blessed with a baby. It would just give the viscount even more control over her, and a child should never be a tool to use against anyone. The viscount already didn't like it, she wasn't residing at his estate and she didn't beg him for funds. It would be far worse if an innocent child had been thrown into that mix of unpleasantness.

She found a maid and told her to have her trunks loaded into the carriage. There was no reason to stay at the manor any longer. She could be at Lady Wyndam's townhouse in half a day if she left soon. At least it was still early enough in the day to leave. It was only a couple hours past dawn, and there was plenty of daylight left for her to travel.

Once she was at Lady Wyndam's townhouse, she would settle in for however long she was to stay there. She didn't stay in one place for long. It made it harder for the viscount to find her and force her back to his estate. So while in London, she rotated residence every fortnight. She always started at Lady Wyndam's and stayed until after the council meeting. Then, a couple of days after that she found a different widow to stay with. At Matron Manor, none of this mattered. No one, except those in the league, knew of its existence. She was always safest there.

Which was why she hated leaving so... It going to be a long few months until she could return again. The carriage was loaded with her trunk so she could depart Matron Manor. She didn't glance back once. Claudine didn't believe in looking backwards at what she couldn't change. It was best to keep moving forward, and to the future—whatever it may hold.

Three

ᏀᏗ

Hudson Lockley, the Earl of Wyndam, tapped his fingers on his knee absent-mindedly. He had been at the country-seat, Wyndam Castle for an extended stay while he met with the estate manager regarding improvements. It had been tedious and had left him in a state of ennui. He would have much rather been in London at his club or even at his townhouse. He had purchased his own residence and left Wyndam House for his grandmother to use. A gentleman needed his own space though and he could always sell it later if or when he needed to.

He should pay a call on his grandmother once he returned to town. She was the only family he had left. The Dowager Countess of Wyndam had raised him. His mother had died in childbirth and his father had used brandy to drown himself in his own grief at her death—then went riding and broke his neck when his horse threw him. Hudson couldn't help being bitter about that. How could a man love a woman so thoroughly he would destroy his own life and abandon his son? He would never fall in love and he certainly would never let a child of his feel as if they didn't matter.

His grandmother had always been his rock. There was no other person he could rely upon more. Even his closest friend, the Duke of Sinbrough, could be too selfish to bother with at times. The Duke of Sin, as many in society dubbed him, had an extravagant personality and believed in surrounding himself with decadence. Hudson was fond of the duke though, and knew if it really mattered, Sinbrough would be there for him. His grandmother was a different story, though. She was a powerhouse of a different sort. All of society respected her, and no one dared to give her the cut direct.

He sighed.

All of these were things he shouldn't let his mind wander over. Hudson had no plans to marry or fall in love. He didn't give one wit about his bloody title or who might inherit it all once he was no longer alive. His grandmother might. She had lost as much as he had. They were both alone in the world. Well, as alone as two people in society could be. Neither of them had someone they could call their own. She had her group of widows she surrounded herself with, and he had a close-knit set of friends he could always rely on. That was something...

He scrubbed his hand over his face. Even now, his boredom couldn't be shaken. He should pay a call on Sinbrough. The duke always had some sort of entertainment at the ready. That might help this restlessness that had settled inside of him. He definitely needed...something. Hudson just didn't know what that something was or could be. He didn't know much of anything anymore. His life was as tedious as that estate business had been. Bloody hell...what a damn mess this all was turning out to be.

The carriage rolled down the road, hitting little juts in the road, periodically making Hudson bounce in his seat. He cursed under his breath. There was no helping that part of travel, either. He had the best carriage available, but unless the roads could be made smoother, he had no choice but to endure it.

It seemed to take forever, but finally, the carriage rolled to a stop in front of his townhouse. He had dubbed it Lockley House since Wyndam House already existed. It had seemed appropriate at the time. He couldn't be certain if the name would remain. Especially if he sold it at some point...

Hudson stepped out of the carriage and walked inside. The servants would see to his trunks. He had other plans. He wanted a bath and then he would depart again. His grandmother would expect him to visit. He'd written he would be returning to London soon, and he always paid a call on her once he was back in town. Hudson would also go to his club. Hopefully Sinbrough would be there and have some inkling of an entertaining pursuit. If the duke wasn't there, then he would pay a call on him at his home. Chances were, he would have his own pursuits there, anyway.

"Carson," Hudson greeted the butler. "I trust everything is well." He spent most of his time in London and had hired a full staff. There were staff at Wyndam Castle as well, but most of the servants remained in London.

"Indeed, my lord," he said. "We received your notice about returning and have prepared for your arrival. "Baldwin has been informed of your return and is already in your chambers. I believe he ordered hot water for a bath."

His valet knew him well. "Wonderful," he said. "I won't be here this evening. Please tell the cook not to prepare a full meal, but I'd like something small after I bathe."

"I will inform her of your instructions." Carson was a stiff older man. He didn't even blink, it seemed. His hair was all white and his eyes so pale a blue they almost seemed translucent. "Will there be anything else you require?"

Hudson shook his head. "That is all."

"I'll have tea and refreshments prepared and sent to your chambers." Carson bowed. "Have a good evening, my lord."

He sure hoped he would. Hudson was eager to leave the townhouse again and go out for the evening. He would visit Wyndam House first, of course. After that, he would be free to do as he pleased. That was another reason not to be encumbered with a wife and family. His devotion to his grandmother was enough for him. If he started to add other individuals into his life, then he wouldn't have that freedom.

Hudson enjoyed his life as it was. There was

definitely no need to make any changes. Then why did he feel as if nothing was right?

CLAUDINE STARED AT THE BOOKS LINING THE SHELVES OF the library. Lady Wyndam had told her to find a book to occupy herself with. None of the books appealed to her. She was far too restless to sit and read. Perhaps she should go for a stroll in the garden. The garden at Wyndam House was lovely. The countess had told her that the gardens at Wyndam Castle were far more extravagant and gorgeous. Claudine couldn't imagine that.

She sighed. Reading was definitely not happening. The library was nice. There were probably a lot of individuals that would be impressed by the collection in Wyndam House. There were too many tomes she would be there for hours, counting them all. There were even a variety of topics to choose from. Anything from proper farming techniques to gothic novels. None of them interested her. She did not need a fictional story to become lost in, and she certainly had no desire to learn how to farm. Her own life was filled with enough to occupy her mind.

Daydreaming or fantasizing would not aid her on the course life had set for her.

She went over to the doors that exited out into the garden. There was a balcony that overlooked the garden and a marble staircase that descended down into it. That balcony was perhaps her favorite part of Wyndam House. She especially loved the section of the garden that had several varieties of roses. There was every color imaginable. It was too bad they hadn't started to bloom yet. It was late March, but they should bud in the next few weeks. Unfortunately, she would most likely be staying at a different residence by then.

Claudine strolled down the staircase. It wasn't too cold out, but it was perhaps chillier than she would have liked. She should have grabbed a spencer or a wrap before venturing outdoors. It was too late now. If she went back inside, then Lady Wyndam might notice her and inquire about her lack of a book.

She stopped by the rose bushes and sighed. If she closed her eyes, she could almost see what they would look like in full bloom. A sea of colors from pink to red to yellow would be everywhere. Perhaps it would be safe enough to visit at least once or twice in the summer months. She reached out and skimmed her hands along the leaves and managed to snag a finger over a thorn. "Ouch," she muttered. That was a brilliant move on her part.

"Are you all right?" a man asked.

Claudine turned and gasped. Who was he? She stayed with Lady Wyndam often enough, but had never encountered an unknown gentleman before. This one was elegantly dressed in all black except for his white shirt and cravat. It wasn't exactly fashionable. There was no other color to be found in his attire. His hair was dark—she couldn't tell if it was a dark shade of brown or just black. Either way, it was striking with his pale blue eyes. "Who are you?" she asked. She didn't address his question. Claudine preferred to give as little information about herself as possible. Especially regarding a gentleman she was not acquainted with.

He lifted a brow and chuckled softly. "You must be one of grandmother's rescues."

She frowned. Grandmother? He must mean Lady Wyndam. "That would make you Lord Wyndam?" She had met the dowager countess a year earlier and had yet to meet her grandson. He always seemed to call on his grandmother when Claudine was otherwise occupied. It wasn't as if she spent all her time at Wyndam House.

"I would be," he said in an arrogant tone. "Who might you be?"

She didn't want to tell him her name. He could be lying about his identity. It was unlikely, but she didn't want to regret anything later. What had he called her earlier? Oh, yes, that's it. "I believe you already know who I am. I'm one of your grandmother's rescues." She mocked his earlier assumption, but Claudine didn't much care. He might be one of the handsomest men she'd ever met, but she owed him nothing. His grandmother, though—she owed her everything.

He laughed. It was loud and boisterous. So glad she could entertain him... "You don't seem like a wounded bird."

What did he mean by that? She narrowed her gaze. "Probably because I am not a bird." If she had wings, she would have flown away from him already. This conversation was odd...

He glanced at her, then studied her. His gaze traveled over her from top to bottom, and it sent shivers down her spine. Her husband had never thoroughly inspected her as this earl just had. "You certainly are not in the traditional sense."

"I am not in any sense," she snapped at him. "Was there a reason you came to the garden?" She wanted him to leave her alone. "Don't you only visit Lady Wyndam briefly, then run away for weeks at a time? Shouldn't you be with her?"

He frowned. "You seem to know my grandmother well." He took a step closer to her. "Do I need to be worried that you're taking advantage of her kindness?"

She rolled her eyes. "As if you would remain at Wyndam House long enough to discover anything that nefarious." He might truly care about his grandmother, but she had never been privy to it.

He stared at her with animosity for several moments. When he did speak, there was a coldness to his tone that sent a different type of shiver down her spine. "Perhaps it is time I took more of an interest in my grandmother's activities then."

Claudine pasted a smile on her face. "How lovely of you to take time out of your busy life to take an interest in your only family. I commend you, my lord." She kept that smile pasted on her face. "I look forward to more visits from you then. If you'll pardon me, I am quite exhausted from my earlier travels. Enjoy your visit."

With those words, she left him alone in the garden. Claudine escaped his presence as fast as possible. Well, as fast as she could without appearing to be running away from him. She didn't want that man to know how he had affected her. She didn't like how her heart had raced at the sight of him or how much she couldn't help wondering what it might be like if he touched her...kissed her... maybe more than that. God help her, Claudine was attracted to Lady Wyndam's grandson.

Four

Hudson tilted his head to the side as he stared after the young woman. She'd surprised him. Few people caught his interest, and this one had done little, and yet, he couldn't be more intrigued. He was certain that had not been her intention; however, she'd succeeded nonetheless. Perhaps he'd have to visit with his grandmother longer than he intended.

He tilted his lips upward into a satisfied smile. She may not have wanted to share her name with him, but he'd have it before the night was concluded. He also wished to know where she'd traveled from... His own travels had made him weary, but he'd still made time to visit with his grandmother. Something he had yet to do...

Hudson sighed. He should quit putting that task off and go to his grandmother's preferred sitting room—where she'd most likely be found at this time of day. Especially if he hoped to extent, his visit and learn more about the beautiful woman he'd just spent a tiny amount of time with. Not nearly enough as he'd have liked to, either.

He strolled toward the stairs that led to the library balcony. Hudson kept a leisurely pace. He was not in any real hurry. Besides, he didn't want his mystery lady to think he was chasing after her. It was best to give her plenty of time to make it inside and out of the library before he entered. To warn her, if she should still be inside the library, he whistled as he climbed the stairs. When he stepped inside the room, it was empty. He couldn't help admitting to himself that he was disappointed. A part of him had hoped she would stay, but then if she had, that would mean a part of her had wanted to spend more time with him. Did she have no interest in him, or was she running scared?

An excellent question and one he would have an answer to soon. He left the library and headed toward his grandmother's sitting room. She sat there in her favorite chair with her cane resting comfortably in her hand. She glance up when he entered and her lips tilted upward into a smile as her gaze met his.

"Hudson," she said in a cheery tone. "I see you made it back to London with no troubles. How are you?"

He grinned back at her. His grandmother never had believed in holding back her thoughts. "It's lovely to see you too," he told her. Hudson walked over and hugged her quickly, then took a seat in the chair directly across from her. "And my trip was uneventful. Which I suppose I should consider a good thing. It would be terrible if I'd been set upon by highway robbers." Though as bored as he'd been, he might have enjoyed a minor scuffle along the way.

"Pfft," she said in a mocking tone. "Don't sass me. I know you too well. You would have thought that a spot of fun."

She knew him too well...it was almost as if she'd been privy to his innermost thoughts. "You don't know that for certain." He couldn't help the grin that spread across his face. "And besides it might have been a jolly time. It's too bad we will never know for certain."

She rolled her eyes. "You know what might actually aid you with that ennui in your life?" His grandmother's gaze seemed to pierce through him.

He was almost afraid to ask. "What?" Hudson actually feared her response. She had such an uncanny ability to cut things to the quick.

"A wife," she said. Then held up her hand, silencing him. "No, I'm not advocating that you marry. I won't ever push for that. I'm just saying that a wife might actually cure what ails you. Your life will never be boring again. There will always be something when there is another person embroiled in your life."

"It's good that you're not insisting I hunt for a bride." He leaned back in his chair. "As I have no intention of doing so."

She smiled. "I expected as much. You're too comfortable in the life you have and there's nothing wrong with that. All I want is for you to be happy."

"I am." He mostly was anyway. "I've been away from London for some time. I thought perhaps I'd stay for dinner if you'll have me." He rarely shared a meal with his grandmother, but it wasn't unheard of. "You can tell me what is new with your life."

"Does that mean I should inform the cook you'll be joining us tonight?" a woman said from the doorway. It wasn't the one he had hoped to see, though.

"Hello, Jules," he greeted his grandmother's companion. Miss Juliet Adams was the reason he didn't worry too much about his grandmother. Juliet ensured she wanted for nothing. If she believed Hudson neglected to visit, she didn't even pause to consider how rude it was to write him and tell him to pay a call. She also hated that he called her Jules, which was why he always did. "Yes. I am going to dine here." He lifted a mocking brow. "Do you always tiptoe around and eavesdrop?"

"Only when you're here," she said. "I try to avoid you if I can."

His lips twitched. "Lovely seeing you, as always."

She ignored him and turned toward his grandmother. "So there will be four of us for the evening meal, then?"

His grandmother nodded. "That's correct."

Hudson turned toward her. "Four?" He lifted a brow. "Who else will be joining us?" This was the perfect opportunity to get his mystery woman's name.

"A good friend of mine," his grandmother told him. "A lovely girl. You must promise to be nice to her. She's had a stressful life and I don't wish to add to it."

"I am always the perfect gentleman," he said as

45

he held his hand over his heart. "When have I even treated a lady wrongly?"

"You haven't," she said, then sighed. "Just promise me."

He frowned. What had this woman gone through to concern his grandmother so? "You have my promise." There wasn't anything else he could say to that. "I look forward to making her acquaintance."

The evening meal would be interesting indeed...

CLAUDINE STARED AT HER GOWN AND HOPED THAT SHE WAS presentable enough for dinner. Her hair was twisted into a simple chignon and her gown was her best, even if it was plain. The evening dress was a pale cream, but the green trim around her waist matched her eyes.

The maid had informed her that Lord Wyndam would join them. She was not thrilled with that piece of news. Would he mention how they had already met in the garden? She certainly hoped not, but she had to be prepared for that to happen. What should she say? Why did this have to be so difficult?

She sighed. There was no more stalling she

could do. She had to leave her bedchamber and go downstairs. They would all be waiting for her to go into dinner, and she was hungry. Claudine left the room and went to the sitting room. She had been right. They were all there waiting for her. The countess hadn't bothered to dress for dinner and neither had Juliet. She felt odd now that she had. Did they not care that an earl was joining them— even if he was Lady Wyndam's grandson? Hell.

"There you are," Lady Wyndam said. "I'd like you to meet my grandson." She gestured toward the earl. "This is Lord Wyndam." She grinned and then nodded in her direction. "Hudson, I'd like you to meet Mrs. Grant."

She hadn't mentioned her given name. Claudine held back a grin at that. Of course she hadn't... Lady Wyndam always showed propriety first—even with her own grandson, apparently. With her father-in-law trying to keep tabs on her, she wouldn't give too many details about her identity out. It was already too much with what she had said. If Lord Wyndam mentioned her name to the wrong person, it might give her location away. She might have to leave the countess's home sooner than planned. Probably right after the meeting of the council...

"It's a pleasure to make your acquaintance," she

said to the earl. "I'm glad you're able to join us for the evening meal."

"Are you?" He lifted a brow.

Was he mocking her? She bet he was... "I am." She smiled at him. She kept it as serene as possible. "I know how much Lady Wyndam misses you when you're away. She must be so pleased you are here with us." Claudine turned toward the countess. "She's always so kind. It's wonderful when that kindness can be returned to her in any fashion."

The countess grinned. "All this talk of my kindness is really too much, dear." She stomped her cane on the floor. "Let's go to the dining room now. I'm famished."

Claudine almost chuckled at her antics. She hadn't lied. The countess was indeed kind, but she was also strong willed and didn't shy from sharing her opinions.

Juliet rose first. "Let me help you." She said to the countess.

"I can see myself in," Lady Wyndam insisted, and tried to push Juliet's hand away. Juliet wasn't having any of it, though.

"For my sake, let me help," Juliet insisted.

"All right, have it your way," the countess grumbled.

They exited the room, leaving Claudine alone with the earl. She should have expected this. How had she failed to see that he'd be left to escort her? He strolled toward her and held out his arm. "My lady," he said. "Allow me to see you to the dining room."

She stared at him longer than she probably should have. He lifted a brow but didn't speak another word. At least not until she looped her arm with his and they started walking... "So Mrs. Grant," he said. "Where is Mr. Grant?"

She frowned. How to answer that question without sounding too sardonic... She had fielded this question in one way or another for over a year now. James had died in battle. It should be easier to say that now, but it still wasn't. She wasn't grieving his loss anymore. She grieved her ideals. When he left to go to war, she'd lost whatever was left of her innocence, and when she found about his death, she'd had to reevaluate everything about her life. "My husband fought bravely at Waterloo," she told him. "So bravely he gave his life to save others...or so I've been told."

"Ah," he said. "I see."

"Do you?" She tilted her head to the side. "What is it that you see?"

"I must confess," he began. "I never quite know what to say when I hear news such as that. I understand how hard it is to speak of such things as I have had my own losses, but in my case, I never knew either of my parents. I feel their loss, and yet I don't. It's hard to feel something you never actually had."

She nodded. "But you still feel that loss, regardless. What would your life have been like even if one of them had lived? It's difficult either way."

"Precisely," he agreed. "Loss is profound no matter how it comes about." He frowned. "Did you love him?" He shook his head. "No, you don't need to answer that. It was rude of me to ask."

She smiled at that. He was not a bad man. How could he be when a woman like Lady Wyndam had raised him? That didn't make him any less of a rake, though. Under the right circumstances, he would willingly seduce her. She was most certain of that fact. "It was rude," she agreed. "And I suppose I did love him or I wouldn't have married him."

"Suppose?" He chuckled lightly. "You are not certain?"

She had to explain herself. Why had she said anything at all? "When James proposed, I was in love with the idea of love," she told him, then paused briefly. "I had an idealistic picture in my mind. He was so handsome in his uniform and I wanted to be his wife. I do believe I cared for him and I his loss hit hard." She tilted her head to the side. "But he left shortly after we said our vows. We never had a chance at a proper marriage and he died before we could ever have that. Sometimes I don't feel as if I were ever married at all." She glanced at him. "Does that make sense?"

"Yes," he said. "Much like my own grief at my parent's loss. It's hard to grasp what that loss meant when I am speaking about something I never truly had."

She nodded. "I suppose you do understand."

Claudine didn't know what else he might have said after that. He pulled out her chair at the table, then took his own seat. The conversation topic took a different turn with Juliet and Lady Wyndam also there. She learned one thing. Proximity only made the earl far more appealing than she liked.

Five

The weather was so beautiful that it took every ounce of Claudine's willpower to walk back inside from the gardens at Wyndam House. She didn't have a choice, though. If she didn't go inside, Lady Wyndam would send a servant out to fetch her. The council meeting was that afternoon and most of the other widows would have arrived already. She had a duty and she would see it through. In a few days, she was leaving Wyndam House and going to stay with Eden, Lady Moreland. She had written Claudine and asked for her assistance preparing her sister-in-law for her debut. Claudine wouldn't attend her ball, but she could help Eden plan the event. It would be nice to be useful until she could return to Matron Manor for an extended stay. She went there more often that any other place, even when it wasn't her turn to be in charge.

She sighed and then walked into Lady Wyndam's sitting room. All of the council had arrived. Claudine had kept them waiting. That was terrible of her, but she couldn't undo it. Lady Covington sat on Lady Wyndam's left and Lady Andover. on her right. Lady Sylvan was on the settee. The only place left for Claudine was next to the marchioness. That was all right with her. She liked Lady Sylvan, and Matron Manor had originally been her estate before she donated it to the Widows' League.

"There you are," Lady Covington said. Her husband had been a viscount. If they were to acknowledge each other by rank, she would be above Claudine, but not anyone else on the council. Claudine was the only one of them that didn't have the rank of lady. That was one reason Lady Wyndam had wanted her on the council. She believed in keeping everything as equal as possible, and as they lost the one woman who didn't hold a title, they wanted a similar woman in her place. "Tea will be here shortly, but I think we can begin. Is there anything new we would like to address first?"

Lady Andover cleared her throat. "We have a new request to join the league."

"Oh?" Lady Sylvan said. "Who would that be?"

They didn't get new additions as often as some might believe. That was a good thing. It was terrible when a woman lost her husband and found themselves without any support. Claudine frowned. There had been maybe one other recruit while she'd been on the council. The rest had already been there or approved to join beforehand. "Who is it?"

Lady Andover's lips twitched. "Elena, the now Dowager Countess of Dryden," she told them. She kept her gaze on Lady Wyndam as she spoke. She couldn't help wondering why. Would Lady Wyndam object to this particular widow?

Lady Wyndam sighed. "I must say, I'm surprised she hasn't been a potential member before now. Lord Dryden was quite a bit older than her."

"He kept hoping you would marry him," Lady Sylvan said. "He believed himself in love with you."

The countess snorted. "He didn't know the meaning of the word. If he loved anyone, it was himself." She sighed. "I am not particularly fond of Lady Dryden, but she is a widow. There is no reason to object to her outright. We have rules in place for a reason. If she breaks them, we will know what to do."

Claudine frowned. "Is that a possibility?"

Lady Covington grinned. "You have never met Lady Dryden, have you?"

Claudine shook her head. That wasn't much of a surprise, though. There were a lot of members of society she had not been introduced to. The Dowager Countess of Dryden wasn't special in that regard. "Should I have?"

"No," Lady Wyndam said. "She's just..."

"More wicked than most," Lady Sylvan supplied.

That made her sound more interesting to her. She didn't know too many wicked people. "Is she?" Claudine lifted a brow. "What does she do to make you say that?"

Lady Sylvan leaned against the settee and stared at Claudine. She didn't say a word for several moments. That made her uncomfortable, but this wasn't the first time the marchioness had studied her as if she didn't understand her. "I forget sometimes how innocent you are." She shook her head. "Did you know that those that are aware of the league consider us wicked widows?"

She nodded. "I've heard some whisper about it."

She didn't think any of the widows were particularly wicked, though. "Why is that?"

"Every widow in the league chooses their own path," Lady Wyndam began. "If you've read through the guidebook, you know some of this."

She nodded. "I've read the entire book." There was some brilliant advice in that book. "Is this with regard to the widows that choose to take a lover?"

Lady Sylvan nodded. "There are many widows that choose that path, and almost all of them decide against remarrying." She gestured between the four other widows. "We are all amongst those widows that chose that path. That doesn't mean that we discourage marriage. If a widow wishes to have a new husband, we support her wholeheartedly."

"As when they choose to just take a lover?" The only man Claudine had ever been with was her husband. Would it be odd to give herself to another man? Immediately, a picture of Lord Wyndam flashed in her mind. That was not a good sign...

"Exactly," Lady Covington said. She nearly beamed at her. "And if a widow remarries, that doesn't mean we will never help her again. She's always welcome at Matron Manor. We're a sisterhood."

"So we're wicked widows because many of us choose to never marry again, but take lovers." She tilted her head to the side. "Perhaps one day I'll be as wicked as many believe I am." Claudine grinned. She would have to think about this and if she really wanted a lover. "I'll have to reread the guidebook."

"You do that." Lady Sylvan's lips twitched. "But if you want some sage advice that isn't there, you come to one of us. We've got more experience between us than a young woman like yourself could ever imagine."

"I'll consider it." And she would... This had given her much to think about. "Now about Lady Dryden..."

"I say invite her," Lady Covington said.

They all agreed and moved on to their next topic. Claudine barely listened to what they discussed and offered little input. She paid enough attention to vote when needed, but her mind was too preoccupied, and one Lord Wyndam was the focus of all that attention. Would he consider having one night with her? And if he did...how did she approach him about it? Claudine wanted him, and she was tired of denying herself. She would find a way to discuss it with him, and soon.

HUDSON SAT IN HIS CLUB AND STARED AROUND HIM. HE had thought coming here would help, but it hadn't. Everything was far too tedious. What was wrong with him? Nothing ever appealed to him anymore. Perhaps he should go somewhere else. A gaming hell or a brothel.

No.

He didn't want just any woman. Hudson wanted Mrs. Grant, and god help him, he didn't even know her given name. That had to be rectified. Especially if he was going to lust after her so thoroughly... He'd much rather say her actual name than her married name. That was so wrong he couldn't even count all the ways... Bloody hell.

"What has you brooding?" The Duke of Sinbrough asked. He had joined Hudson at the club. His black hair was disheveled and his green eyes had a haziness to them. How much had the duke had to drink already? They had ordered another decanter for brandy, but Sinbrough had imbibed most of it. Hudson couldn't even muster an interest in some excellent brandy.

"Nothing," he said. The Duke of Sin wouldn't

understand that Hudson wanted one woman. To the duke any woman would do. He loved all women. Particularly if they were naked and willing to spend time in his bed... Hudson had always been more discerning than his friend.

"Sinbrough," a gentleman said from behind Hudson. "I didn't expect to find you here."

"Caufield," the duke greeted. "How are you, old friend? I thought you were rusticating at your father's estate." The Marquess of Caufield sauntered over. His brown hair was neat and tidy, and his brown eyes as clear as Sinbrough's were hazy.

"I am here on business. I don't expect to be in town long," Caufield dropped into an empty seat next to the duke. He turned toward Hudson and nodded. "How is everything with you?"

"The same." Nothing ever changed. That was part of his problem. "What business brings you to town?" It wasn't done to partake in actual business, but the dukedom Caufield would inherit one day had been in dire straits. His father had done what was necessary to make it flush again, and he expected his only son to help him keep it that way. Hudson actually respected both of them more for their hard work.

"Father is looking at acquiring a shipping company. He asked me to meet with them and determine if it is a sound investment." Caufield shrugged. "I have a meeting with the Marquess of Savorton in the morning."

Savorton Shipping was an enormous empire. As far as Hudson knew, they were quite prosperous too. "Are you buying their entire line?"

He shook his head. "No, just a few of their smaller ships. It's a branch of their company that they already established and don't use as much anymore. They've grown too big for the smaller vessels." Caufield gestured to a servant to visit their table. "I need to determine if it's worth our time to take it off their hands."

Hudson nodded. "I hope it is a worthwhile endeavor, then."

The servant came over to the table and Caufield greeted him. "Bring me a glass and another decanter of brandy." The servant nodded and then left to fetch what the marquess had ordered. The marquess turned his attention back to them. "I hope so as well. It will be the first company my father will leave solely to my supervision if we buy it. I look forward to the challenge."

"You'll do bloody fantastic with it," Sinbrough told him. "How long are you in town?"

"A sennight at least," he said. "But probably a month if we decide to purchase the ships."

"Good," Sinbrough said. "Then I'll have to have a party to celebrate. The sooner the better, since you might not be here long. We can always have another one if need be."

Hudson grinned. Sinbrough's parties were not the normal ton fair. They were far more risqué and were usually a masquerade of some sort. That allowed some of the more virtuous ladies to attend and keep their reputation intact. He lifted his glass of brandy. "I think I can drink to that."

Caufield laughed. "I will as well." The servant had dropped off another decanter of brandy and a glass. The marquess had just finished filling it and held it up toward them. "To pleasant entertainments with friends."

They all took a drink of their brandy. It burned as it slid down Hudson's throat. He always enjoyed that particular burn. The only thing better was a good Scottish whiskey. "What kind of party do you plan on having?" He knew the answer, or thought he did, but wanted confirmation. Could he lure Mrs. Grant to Sinbrough's masquerade?

"There's only one kind of ball to host," Sinbrough said. "As you well know."

"A masquerade," Caufield said. They all knew what the duke liked. Their friendship went back to their days at Eton. "Send my invitation to my town-house. I'll definitely attend." He finished his brandy. "But I am afraid I must depart. I have some early meetings in the morning."

"You're far too boring these days," Sinbrough told the marquess. "Wyndam isn't much better. Though at least he is around more for me to complain to."

Caufield chuckled. "You're lucky he allows it." He nodded at them both. "Have a good evening." Then with those words he turned around and left Hudson and Sinbrough alone.

"I hate to be the bearer of bad news, but I must leave as well. I promised my grandmother I'd pay a call on her." Hudson hadn't, but he had no desire to stay.

"This late?" Sinbrough frowned.

"It's not that late," Hudson said defensively. It might be, but he still didn't care. It wasn't his grand-mother he wished to visit, regardless. "Don't drink too much brandy. You'll want to be able to find your way home. Good evening." Hudson didn't give him time to object. He walked away from the duke briskly. There was a young widow he wished to see, and the duke just didn't compare to her allure. He grinned as he exited his club. He couldn't wait to see his Mrs. Grant.

Six

Hudson strolled into the garden behind Wyndam House. This might be the biggest mistake he'd ever made, but he still hadn't turned back. What the hell was he thinking? He shook his head and continued forward. He could just stay in the garden for a little while instead of actually going inside the house. What would his excuse be for arriving so late? His grandmother would think he'd lost his bloody mind. This was an insane idea after all...

He sighed.

What should he do? He wandered over to the bench near the rose garden, then stopped and stared. There she was. Had he conjured her by thinking of her? The roses were not even in bloom yet. Why was she sitting out there staring at the bushes as if she could will them to sprout roses? He should go now before she saw him. He frowned. But isn't she the very reason he'd come to Wyndam House? If he left now, then he might miss his chance.

Hudson took a step back but stepped on something that sent a cracking sound around him. He cursed under his breath. If he'd hoped to escape without her noticing him, then he'd failed. She turned at the sound and her gaze found his. The moon had the audacity to be full and bright, too. There wasn't much that light hid in the surrounding darkness. There was nothing for it. He would have to move forward and hope he didn't appear to be a complete dolt.

"Lord Wyndam," she greeted him. "Do you always enter by way of the garden?" Her brow lifted in a questioning manner.

"I like the gardens here," he said, as if that had answered her question. His lips twitched in amusement. "It appears you do as well."

She tilted her head to the side as if studying him. "They are lovely. More so later in spring and summer." She sighed. "It's a pity I'll miss that."

She was leaving? He couldn't allow that to

happen. He would miss his chance with her if she did. "Where will you go?" He couldn't make her stay even if he wanted to, but he could perhaps discover her location to use later.

"Many places," she said. What kind of answer was that? She shrugged. "I don't have a home. At least not one I wish to claim." She smiled, but it didn't seem to reach her eyes. "You might say I'm a lost soul constantly wandering without one place, any place to be rooted to."

What was he supposed to say to that? There was no flirtation that could make light of her words. He couldn't help her, even if he wanted to. This was beyond his capabilities. "How often to you visit with my grandmother?"

"As often as I need to." She stood. "Did you come to Wyndam House for a particular reason?"

He stepped closer to her. It was more of a compulsion than anything. Hudson needed to be near her. Something about her called to him. He wanted to place his palm on her cheek and trail his fingers across her lips. Then, if she allowed him to, he wanted to slant his lips over hers and kiss her until their breaths mingled. He wanted to breathe her in until he didn't know where he started and she ended. "I came for you." His voice was husky as he spoke. "It was a foolish thing to do, but I couldn't help myself."

Her lips parted, and she stared at him. No words seemed necessary between them. She closed her eyes and inhaled, then blew it out slowly. When she opened her eyes, she seemed more in control. He didn't like that one bit. "You shouldn't be here."

"And yet I am." He could set aside their earlier conversation. It had been too deep for what he hoped to have with her. There was no place in his life for lost souls. Only mutual pleasure and no promises of a future... He couldn't offer anyone the latter. "Don't make me go."

"I can't even if I wanted to." She lifted her chin defiantly. "It is technically your house."

"But you don't want to." Her words were not lost on him. She wanted him to stay. "If we're to be close, don't you think we should use our given names with each other?" He refused to call her Mrs. Grant. "Please call me Hudson."

She shook her head. "That's far too familiar, my lord," she told him. "That's not the nature of our relationship."

"It is if we choose it to be." He kept his tone light and hoped he enticed her to his way of thinking. She was so lovely it stole his breath to gaze upon her. "What's your name, love?"

"You don't know my name, so you're going to resort to endearments." She sounded amused. That was a good sign, wasn't it? "What will you call me next, I wonder?"

"I'd like to call you mine," he said before he could stop himself. "Sweetness. Tell me your name."

She shook her head. "It is a terrible idea. There can never be anything between us."

How could he convince her that there could be? She didn't seem to want any promises from him any more than he could give them. She had already been married once and lost the man she had loved. If anyone understood the emotions loss brought, she would. He never wanted to love another and risk the chance he might lose them. He'd already lost so much and he refused to lose the love of his life. Not that she was that for him...he didn't even want to look for love, let alone allow it to find him.

He moved to her side and cupped her cheek. Could he kiss her? Would she allow it? Hudson leaned down until his lips hovered just above her. The sharp intake of her breath sent shivers down his spine. She hadn't pushed him away. He decided to take a chance and pressed his lips to hers. It was the lightest of kisses, but it was the most shocking of his life. The simplicity of it was everything and nothing at the same time. He stepped back, stunned. What had just happened?

"All right," she said, then licked her lips. "You win."

Had he? "What is my boon?"

"My name is Claudine," she told him. She didn't give him a chance to respond. Claudine walked away from him and went inside the house. He didn't think she was right. He hadn't won a thing. Yes, she told him her name, but he feared she'd stolen something from him. Something he hadn't wanted to give, and it was all hers...his heart.

CLAUDINE DIDN'T KNOW WHAT HAD GOTTEN OVER HER. She should not have allowed him to get so close to her. Lord Wyndam might prove to be her undoing. She wanted to throw her arms around him and kiss him far more passionately than that kiss had been. It had been chaste, and it had excited her far more than her husband's ever had. This was a disaster. She shouldn't have told him her name, either. It had all been too much.

"What has you so flushed?"

She jumped at the sound of Juliet's voice. How had she sneaked up on her? Was she that lost in her own thoughts? "You scared me."

"My apologies," she said. "I hadn't meant to. I came to return this book and find something new." She pushed the tome onto a shelf. "Were you outside?"

Claudine nodded. Should she tell Juliet about Hudson's visit? She wanted to think about him as Lord Wyndam, but the more she thought about it, the more she couldn't. He would forever be Hudson to her now. "Yes," she said. "I find the garden calming." At least she had until Hudson's visit.

"They are lovely," Juliet agreed. "I enjoy them myself. It had to be cold out there, though. Your cheeks are quite red."

Claudine doubted the cold had anything to do with the state of her reddened cheeks. She had to talk to someone. Juliet wasn't a widow, but she might still understand. "How well do you know Lord Wyndam?"

Juliet blinked several times. Had her question caught the woman off guard? She opened her mouth and closed it several times. When she spoke, there was a carefulness to her tone. "Have you taken a fancy to him?"

Claudine shook her head. "No, I mean I don't know." She sighed. "He may have taken one to me."

Juliet nodded thoughtfully. "He is handsome and charming. He adores his grandmother and would do anything for her. I think that says a lot about him deep down." She tilted her head to the side. "He's never flirted with me, and that is not me being vain. To him, I am an extension of his grandmother and therefore I am accorded a certain amount of respect. He teases me like I might be his sister or another family member."

"What does that have to do with me?" Claudine was confused. What was Juliet trying to say?

"It didn't escape my notice how he watched you." Juliet shrugged lightly. "You're a guest, but not his grandmother's companion. You are not off limits."

"So you believe he would be interested in an affair with me?" Claudine was not certain how that made her feel. Did she want more than that with him? No. She didn't have to think too long about it. She'd already been married, and it hadn't gone at all as she had imagined. Marriage was not something that she would ever do rashly again.

"I think the question is, what do you want with him?" Juliet smiled. "You're the one asking questions. What are you hoping for?"

Claudine nibbled on her bottom lip. A week ago she would have been emphatic about what she didn't want and that was a man of any kind for any reason. She didn't hate men; she just didn't want to allow one to have any control over her life again. Now though... Having an affair of some sort wouldn't be giving away anything. It would be, hopefully, gaining something she had never had. A lover sounded fantastic. She had been skimming some of the guidebook and the advice of widows before her. A lot of them hadn't had wonderful marriages and taking a lover had changed things for them. The right man could be wonderful to have for a brief time in her life, and Hudson might be the one that could do that for her.

"I don't know what I want." That was true for the most part. "He was here a few moments ago."

"Was he?" There was amusement mixed with curiosity in her tone. "How unusual for him." She grinned. "He likes you far more than even I realized. Though I don't think he had his grandmother fooled."

"What?" Lady Wyndam had picked up on his

interest in Claudine? That couldn't be good. No. She didn't like it at all. "What did she say?"

"You know the countess. She never says much. It is what she does that you have to take notice of. She wouldn't be against a match between you and her grandson." Juliet frowned. "But she also knows the two of you well enough that she suspects it won't happen. You're both against marriage for your own reasons."

"Surely she doesn't think...." She shook her head. "She knows I don't wish to remarry."

"She does," Juliet confirmed. "And Lord Wyndam has been vocal about remaining unwed himself. That doesn't mean she doesn't wish for him to find love and happiness. She adores you. Two of her favorite people together...that's the stuff dreams are made of."

Claudine didn't want to give Lady Wyndam false hope. She loved her grandson and she couldn't get between them in any way. Having an affair with him would be a terrible idea. It didn't matter if it would make her feel better. Some things were far more important. Her relationship with the countess was one of them. "Then that settles things." She blew out a breath. "I know what to do."

"I hope so," Juliet said in a solemn tone. "And I

hope that it isn't what I think. You deserve happiness, too." She snatched a book off the shelf, then walked over to Claudine. "Even if it is short-lived. Take a chance with the earl. I do believe you won't regret it."

With those words, she exited the library. Claudine had much to consider. Juliet was wrong, though. If she took Hudson as a lover, she might come to regret it. If she took that leap, she wanted to make sure she could live with the consequences.

Seven

◠◡◠

Claudine stared out the window in Eden's sitting room. She had moved to the Moreland townhouse a few days earlier. She would stay with the Countess of Moreland until it was time for her to return to Matron Manor in a few weeks. Claudine had one more meeting with the council before she could take up residence there again. When she returned, she wouldn't be the widow in charge, but she could still enjoy the freedom of being there. So far her father-in-law hadn't realized she had returned to London, and she wanted to keep it that way. While at Matron Manor, there was no danger of him locating her.

If he happened to find her, nothing terrible

would happen. They would just have another one of their awful disagreements. He would try to order her to return to Artcrest Abbey. She didn't hate the Viscount of Artcrest, but he wasn't exactly a pleasant man either. Being around her husband's father had given her a lot of insight as to why James had made some decisions he had.

They'd married in Scotland since they had been near the border and he hadn't told his father until afterward. Though he must have trusted the viscount somewhat. He had made him Claudine's guardian in the event of his death. That was why the viscount wouldn't leave her alone to make any decisions for her own life. He thought he knew better than she did. He might be many years older than her, but that did not make him wiser. She would not allow him to dictate to her.

Of course, moving around often was not a good life plan, but for now, it worked for her. There was a clause that would give her control of her life again. She would either have to remarry, which wasn't control at all, or wait until she reached her thirtieth year. Unfortunately, that was still many years away, and she had no intention of saying wedding vows ever again. So, she kept herself hidden. She hated drama, and it seemed the best solution for her.

"All right," Eden said as she strolled into the room. "Caden is settled in the nursery with the nanny, and Roslyn had retired to her bedchamber. She claims she has a headache, but I think she doesn't want to socialize with us."

"Does she consider us to be too stuffy then?" Claudine lifted a brow and chuckled. "We must be old matrons by now then."

Eden sighed. "She's not that much younger than we are. There is only three years between us. She would have already had a debut season if we didn't have to observe a mourning period after William's death."

Claudine frowned. "Is she in a hurry to find a husband, then?" Someone should tell the young lady that marriage is not something to be taken lightly. She wished someone had taken her aside and explained more to her. Maybe then she wouldn't have rushed to the altar with James. "

Eden shook her head. "No." She sat down on the settee. "Roslyn wants a season. She longs to dance and make friends. I'm not sure she cares if she ever marries. But the parties..." Eden blew out a breath. "That she cannot wait for. It all seems exciting to her. As I never had a season, I suppose I understand that."

Claudine nodded. "It must seem like a different world to her." She sat down on the chair near the settee. "I've never attended a ball myself. I wonder if that is why I accepted the first gentleman that offered for me. Would I have married James if I had other choices?"

"I never was given a choice. My father decided on my marriage for me and I was to do as I was told." She shrugged. "I believed he was doing what was best for me. Only now do I question that. I don't want Roslyn to feel as if she had no choices. She doesn't have any other family but Caden, and me, and well, he is two. He can't make her do anything." She chuckled lightly. "She won't have to marry anyone unless she truly wants to, and no one is going to force her to do anything."

"It's good she has you to protect her." What Claudine didn't say was that neither of them had that. They both should have, but they'd been let down by their own family members. Only someone that had been through something similar as they had would understand that. The widows' league had given them a group of women that they could rely on, and that had been the saving grace of many women.

Eden blew out a breath. "I do hope she comes to realize that one day."

"She will," Claudine said, with conviction in her tone. "She may never actually acknowledge it, but she will understand."

"I suppose that may be true." She tapped her finger on the side of the settee. "There's something else I wanted to discuss with you now that we are alone," Eden began. "I have to tell you about a ball I've been invited to." She glanced around the room as if ensuring they were alone. "It's not a normal sort of ball."

"What do you mean not the normal sort?" Claudine sat up straighter and stared at Eden. "What other type of ball is there?"

"Well, there are a lot of different types depending on themes..." She waved her hand dismissively. "This one is a masquerade."

"Oh..." She slumped back down. "That's not so different."

"It is when the host is the Duke of Sinbrough." Eden practically hissed out that last bit of news. "His masquerades are very risqué."

Claudine frowned. "Are you going?"

"I don't know..." Eden nibbled on her bottom lip.

"I've considered it and I read through the guidebook again, and I might consider taking a lover."

"Have you?" Claudine lifted a brow. She had been considering that very thing herself. Though she had a certain gentleman in mind if she decided on a lover. "When is this masquerade?"

"In two nights," Eden said. "I would like for you to go with me. I might need someone there..." She closed her eyes a moment and took a deep breath, then opened them. "I'm too nervous to go by myself. Will you attend with me? I know it's asking a lot. Especially with your concerns about Viscount Artcrest... But since we'll be wearing masks..."

Claudine wanted to say no, but she wouldn't. Eden needed her. "I'll attend."

Eden clapped her hands excitedly. "Fabulous. I'll arrange everything. Even our costumes. This will be a spectacular evening."

She had her doubts, but Claudine wouldn't deflate her friend's excitement. Perhaps it would be as wonderful as Eden hoped. Neither one of them would know until that evening.

HUDSON SAT IN THE DUKE OF SINBROUGH'S STUDY listening to his friend plan his upcoming masquerade. There were probably better uses for his time, but he couldn't think of any just then. In fact, there was only one thing he could think of on repeat —Claudine.

That kiss had perhaps been the chastest in his entire life, but nothing had ever excited him more than her lips beneath his. Hudson wanted another opportunity to kiss her, but this time, he would taste her fully. He was shocked he had not done it that night. He couldn't stop thinking about her and what he should have done. It was a loop that repeated over and over again.

"Are you even listening to me?" Sinbrough asked.

"Of course, Your Grace," Hudson said in a droll tone. "Masquerade. Decorations. Musicians." He rolled his hand in a dismissive tone. "All intriguing..."

"You're a cad," the duke said. "And a terrible friend."

"The worst," Hudson agreed. "Does that mean I am no longer invited?"

Sinbrough snorted. "I should rescind your invitation, but I won't. I'm a forgiving sort, after all."

Hudson yawned. "So forgiving," he agreed. He should ask the duke to invite Claudine. Would she even attend? If she was aware of the type of party the duke threw, she might avoid it. She was not a scandalous sort of woman. She may be a widow, but that didn't mean she would be willing to attend a masquerade that was quite lewd at times. "I'm fortunate to have such a congenial and well-intentioned friend as you."

"Damn right you are," the duke said. "I invited a few new widows to this one."

"Say what?" Hudson sat up straighter at the duke's announcement. His brandy sloshed around in his glass and he'd nearly spilled it. "What new widows?" Had he met Claudine? He sure as hell hoped not. A lot of women fell willingly into the duke's arms and if he had his way with Claudine, he might have to hurt his friend.

"The Countess of Moreland, for one," the duke said. "Her husband was the worst sort of scoundrel. She deserves to have a bit of fun, and since she's out of mourning, I thought perhaps she might enjoy a good masquerade."

Hudson tilted his head to the side. Had he ever met Lady Moreland? He didn't think he had. "Are there any other widows?"

"The Countess of Dryden," he said. "Though she is more recently widowed. I don't think she'll care much for propriety. I've heard she's into all things decadent."

"Ah," he said. "I'm acquainted with that widow." The Earl of Dryden had been his guardian when he was a boy. He'd been to his wedding when he married his young bride. He had been a good thirty years her senior. It was clear he had only married the young lady to get his heir, and she hadn't appeared thrilled with the marriage. After she had given birth to the heir, she had kept her distance from her elderly husband. There were a lot of rumors about her taking many lovers, though he didn't know if any of it was true. "She'll likely attend the masquerade."

"But not Lady Moreland?" Sinbrough lifted a brow. "You may be right. I'm not acquainted with either lady, but I do hope to rectify that."

"Then I do hope both attend." Hudson sipped his brandy. There was only one widow he had an interest in. He didn't want to ask the duke to invite her, though. He might take a personal interest in Claudine, and that was the last thing Hudson wanted. "I on the other hand don't have anything in particular I am expecting from this masquerade. I've learned to just show up and throw myself into the festivities. It's much more entertaining that way."

Sinbrough chuckled. "I can't disagree with you. I love spontaneity."

It was something they had all lived by for many years now. It might have gotten to be part of his ennui lately, though. What should have helped alleviate any sense of boredom only added to it. He could be wrong though. Perhaps he was just tired of all the constant activity. Hudson didn't know why he felt so listless lately.

In fact, there had only been a handful of times he hadn't felt that way. Claudine had been at the center of it all. Was she the answer to everything? That couldn't be right. He was probably overthinking it all.

"I trust that you'll plan the best masquerade." He stood and swallowed the contents of his glass. The brandy burned as it traveled down his throat. "And you can count on my attendance." He set his empty glass on the table. "Do let me know if I can be of assistance. If not, I'll see you in a couple of nights at the masquerade. I have some plans of my own to make." Like how to ensure that Claudine would be at this ball the duke planned. "Good evening." Hudson nodded at his friend and left the study.

He did not know yet how he would make it all happen, but he would. First, he would have to pay a call on his grandmother, and in turn, Claudine. When he saw her, inspiration would strike. At least he prayed it would...

Eight

Claudine stared at the costume that Eden had procured for her and frowned. It had a far more daring cut on it than anything she had ever worn. It was a pale pink gown that was almost the same shade as her skin—almost as if she wore nothing at all at a glance. The skirt had an overlay of delicate lace that floated over the chiffon material. The bodice had been cut low enough that if she bent the wrong way, her décolletage might topple out of the top. There was a ribbon just underneath the bodice in a darker shade of pink. Like a little bow wrapping up a present for just the right person...

There was only one gentleman she wished to have see her in that gown. Would he be at the masquerade? She'd heard a rumor he was a friend of the Duke of Sinbrough. That meant he would likely have an invitation to attend. How would she find him in a sea of masks, though? Claudine didn't have the faintest idea how to navigate the debauched waters of one of the Duke of Sin's masquerades.

She sighed and held up the gown. Was she really going to do this? Claudine nibbled on her bottom lip and then closed her eyes. Yes. She would go to the masquerade with Eden. She'd made a promise to her, and she did hope to cross paths with the Earl of Wyndam. When she did, then she'd have a decision to make. Would she approach him about having one night of seduction or would she shy away from what she wanted?

"What do you think of it?" Eden asked from the doorway to Claudine's bedchamber.

"You don't think it is a bit..."

"Naughty?" Eden supplied. "Wicked?"

Claudine laughed. "We are a couple of wicked widows, aren't we?" She set the gown on her bed and picked up the masque. It was pure white except for the pink feathers that matched her gown. There was also a pink ribbon to tie the mask and keep it secured on her face. She preferred this style to the masks with handles on them. She would much prefer to have her hands free for the evening. Also, she didn't really want to remove the mask. Whatever she could do to keep her identity concealed, the better.

"We definitely will embrace our wicked side tonight." Eden trailed her fingers over Claudine's gown. "Mine is just as daring as yours. I chose a different shade, though."

"Oh?" Claudine lifted a brow. "What color is it?"

"It's pure white." She grinned. "Like a debutante preparing for her first ball." Eden winked. "Do you think the scoundrels of the ton will be drawn to my projected innocence?"

Claudine groaned. "I thought the pale pink of my gown was going to draw them all to me, but you're right. They're going to wonder what woman would wear white to a ball of debauchery."

Eden giggled. "It's going to be such fun." She twirled around the room. "I cannot wait until it begins." She sighed. "But first I must start preparing. I've ordered a bath for both of us. They should bring the tub up shortly to your chamber. Emily is going to assist you with your preparations."

"That sounds lovely," Claudine said. "I've never been to any sort of ball before. I'm a little anxious.

Especially since this isn't the normal sort of gathering for members of the ton."

"I've attended a few balls." She wrinkled her nose. "But I never had a debut season. What I've noticed from those that I've been privy to—you're not missing much. I am glad you'll be here to help with Roslyn's season, though. I sorely need a friend to lean on."

Claudine was glad to help her. She wasn't sure how she felt about hiding from society still, though. She wished that the viscount would leave her to live her life as she chose to. Perhaps one day he would see reason, but until then she'd continue as she had been for the past year. As long as he couldn't force her to his country estate, she would be all right. So far he hadn't gone so far as to do that.

"I'll be here as long as I can be," she told her. Any widow Claudine worked close with knew that she couldn't always stay very long. She didn't explain why to too many people. The more a widow knew, the more she could accidentally give away. She didn't want to put any of the widows in a position they might feel uncomfortable in. In time, she would find a solution to her issue. Even if it meant she might have to leave the country. Though she would like to avoid that possibility...

"I'll leave you to your preparations. I'll meet you in the foyer before we're scheduled to depart." Eden smiled at her. "I have a good feeling about this evening."

"I do too." Claudine had been unsure when she had first gazed upon that scandalous gown, but now she felt the same way that Eden did. She would have a grand time at the masquerade. At least she hoped she would. It would be far better if Hudson were there. She would have her one night with her rogue. Even if it didn't happen at the masquerade. She just didn't know how she would make it happen outside of this particular event. Would she have to call on him? Send him a missive? She hadn't any idea how to schedule an assignation. This was completely out of anything she had ever experienced. "Now go. You have your own bath and preparations to complete."

Eden laughed and then left the room. Claudine glanced back at that gown and let out a breath. It would be an interesting evening, no matter what. It was time she started to truly live her life. Just because her husband had died didn't mean she should stop living. She was content with her decision, and soon, hopefully, she'd feel a hell of a lot more than that.

HUDSON DIDN'T WEAR A COSTUME TO THE MASQUERADE. He never did. Oh, he had a mask, and he did put it on, but that was the extent of what he did to prepare. He didn't see any reason to go out of his way for these balls that Sinbrough hosted. At least he didn't stand out in the crowd with his lack of costume. He wasn't the only gentleman dressed in nearly all black and a mask.

The ladies, on the other hand stood out. They wanted an individuality that would spark the interest in the men in attendance. Every lady seemed to wear something both scandalous and vibrant. Like a bunch of birds trying to attract a mate. The more outlandish the gown, the more likely they might catch the attention of a gentleman to spend their evening with.

All of that had appealed to Hudson in the past. He found that this time he couldn't find one lady that interested him. They all seemed overly done and off-putting. It probably wasn't them, though. He only wanted one woman, and she seemed so far out of reach it was frustrating. Would she be willing to have an affair with him? Would that be enough for him? What exactly was he hoping for with Claudine?

He cursed and ran his finger through his hair. This wasn't helping him at all. Perhaps he should leave and consider this evening a failure. He had attended, hoping he would find another woman to catch his attention. None of them had. The very idea of touching any of them left a sick feeling in his stomach. They were not her. They were not Claudine. What was it about her that drew him? He couldn't say even if he tried, and he wasn't sure he wanted to.

"Brooding in the corner like a wallflower isn't doing you any favors," Sinbrough said as he stepped beside him.

"Bugger off," Hudson told him. "I don't need any advice from you."

"That wasn't advice, you bloody wanker," Sinbrough said, and then laughed. "I was stating a fact. There are many birds ready to be plucked here tonight. Pick one, hell pick several to join you in this little corner. It'll be far more entertaining that way."

Hudson rolled his eyes. For the Duke of Sinbrough, his solution was simple. There was nothing complicated about picking a beautiful woman and finding some pleasure. It was what he did, and he made no apologies for it. Sinbrough enjoyed being a little out of control. He lived for that spontaneity. It didn't get any simpler than that. Hudson wished he could be like Sinbrough at times. But he couldn't let go long enough to fully embrace a full life of sin like the duke did.

"I don't want any of them," he said. "They don't appeal to me."

Sinbrough laughed. Then stared at him, a little stunned. "Oh, you meant that. Truly?" He shook his head. "What isn't appealing? They're all beautiful."

He shrugged. "That's not enough for me anymore." God help him, he wanted to like a woman he bedded.

"Hell," Sinbrough said. "You're cursed, aren't you? That's the only thing that makes sense. Please tell me that grandmother of yours hasn't convinced you to." He shuddered. "take a wife." He said the last bit as if he'd eaten something distasteful.

Hudson laughed. "You know my grandmother. You even like her." He met the duke's gaze. "When has she ever suggested I find a wife?"

"My apologies," he said with sincerity. "It was just the only thing that made sense. You have never been so discerning that you don't find one woman here appealing."

Everything came back to Claudine. She was the only woman he wanted. That might change in time, but at this particular moment, it was his truth. "I cannot explain it."

"Then don't try." The duke frowned. "You might not find any of them to your liking, but I have no such difficulties. There are several I do hope to have before the night is over."

Hudson grinned. He doubted his friend would ever change. He liked women too much to choose just one. If one ever did, she would have to be one hell of a woman. She would have to be to keep the duke's interest forever. He sure hoped Sinbrough met such a woman. It would be entertaining to watch his downfall. "That doesn't surprise me. Who do you plan on seducing first?"

"I haven't decided." The duke wiggled his eyebrows. "But the lady in white that just entered is definitely intriguing." Then he tilted his head to the side. "And her companion is welcome to join us."

Who wore white to one of these masquerades? That was definitely a change. There were a lot of reds, greens, and blues... but white? That was out of character for the ladies that Sinbrough invited. "Are they new?"

The other lady wore a pink gown. At least he

thought it was pink... It was the same shade as the lady's skin. If he couldn't make out the shape of her gown in the candlelight, he would wonder if she had anything on at all.

"Perhaps," the duke said. "I did invite a few new widows. Should we introduce ourselves?"

Hudson frowned. He was curious. "All right, you convinced me. Let's cross over to the ladies." Perhaps they were cleverer than the rest of the ladies in attendance. Their attire was certainly unexpected.

The duke did not reply. Instead, he started toward the two ladies. Hudson followed behind him. He could wait until they reached them to speak again. The two of them kept a brisk pace until they were at the ladies' sides. They both glanced up at their approach. The bodices of their gowns were cut low. Something they couldn't tell from the other side of the room. That made that pink gown even more daring. How interesting...

Hudson lifted his gaze and met hers, then smiled. It was her. He didn't need her to remove that mask to know for sure. Claudine had come. Had she received his invitation? He'd sent it to his grandmother's but had learned later she'd left. Had it been forwarded to her?

She smiled at him, and it warmed him from the

inside out. "My lord," she said, and then curtsied. It gave him a lovely view of her décolletage.

Hudson held out his arm. "Dance with me." He didn't ask her. He wouldn't have taken no for an answer. This was an opportunity he would not miss. They would dance. They might do more. Either way, he would have her in his arms even for a few brief moments of the waltz.

Thankfully, Claudine didn't argue. She allowed him to lead her onto the floor. He was twirling her around, not listening to the strands of the music. His focus was completely on her, and what he wanted. It was almost magical...

Nine

This had to be the most magical moment of her life...

Claudine stared up at him and allowed herself to become lost in the moment. She had hoped he would be at the masquerade, but hadn't dared to believe he truly would attend. How serendipitous that they had found each other nearly immediately upon her arrival. Fate must have meant for them to spend this night together. If she had wondered before if she should approach him about one night of passion together, she didn't any longer. She wanted him. Claudine would have one night with the rogue of her choosing, and her desire for Hudson surpassed anything she'd ever experienced in her entire life.

He twirled her around the floor with ease. Claudine had learned all the proper steps to dances, but she'd had no opportunity to actually use those lessons. She suspected even if she hadn't held rudimentary skills, he'd have led her into the dance with ease. He danced quite gracefully, and equally as masterfully. This was a moment in time she would never forget. She would replay this dance over and over in her mind and never tire of reliving it. If she could make it last longer, she would. It was that magical of a moment. One that should be preserved in any way possible...

She was so lost in the dance Claudine didn't realize when he led her toward the very edge of the floor. There, he brought them to a stop and led them away from those engrossed in their own dances. He stopped before a pair of doors that had glass panes, allowing a person to view the gardens outside. He opened the doors, and they exited the ballroom. The balcony wasn't empty, but it wasn't nearly as crowded as the dance floor.

They didn't speak as they walked away from the other guests. He took her hand in his and led her to a staircase. They always seemed to find themselves together in a garden. It was a good thing that she adored gardens. "Where are we going?" she asked.

"Anywhere I can be alone with you," he answered.

Claudine was quite all right with that plan. She would walk faster if that would aid her in finding such a place. The masquerade was a crush by society's standards. Had everyone been invited? Even those too prudish to admit they even felt desire? A mask did give a person a certain amount of anonymity. That might make an individual feel more at ease at such events. She suspected that was why the duke always held a masquerade instead of a normal sort of ball.

"Do you know where you're going?" She was eager to be alone with him. Her curiosity had always been one of her downfalls.

"I do," he said. "I promise we will be completely alone soon. No one knows of this place." He grinned. "In this instance, it helps to know the duke and his home well."

She was grateful that he knew a place they could be alone. She suspected inside the duke's home it would be impossible to find such a place. What would the other guests do? Would they give into their desire even though they might have an audience? She shivered. That was truly scandalous, and why did the very idea of someone viewing her passionate encounters thrill her? She'd never had such wicked ideas before. Had she turned into such a wanton creature, or had she always been this way? Perhaps it was being with Hudson that had changed her. He'd barely kissed her and already she seemed like a true, wicked widow.

"Here we are," he said. They arrived at a conservatory that wasn't attached to the main house. It was at the far back of the gardens and to reach it, they had to walk through a maze, or what seemed like a maze. She doubted anyone could navigate that path if they had not taken it many times already.

Hudson lifted a latch hidden behind a large rock and retrieved a key. He slid it in the lock and turned it, then opened the door. He bowed. "My lady," he said. "Will you enter with me?"

She grinned. "I suppose I trust you enough to go inside."

Claudine went through the entrance and he followed behind her, chuckling. She turned around and met his heated gaze. He shut the door and then turned the lock. "We don't want anyone to interrupt us." He slid the key into his pocket. "And without this they'll have to break some glass to gain entry." His grin turned wicked. "No one would dare incur the duke's wrath by doing that."

"I don't suppose they would." She glanced away from him and then walked farther into the conservatory. There were many plants inside, and some roses were already in full bloom. How did the duke manage this? Perhaps she would ask him some day. She leaned down and inhaled. The scent was wonderful. "I think I could spend days in here."

Hudson stepped behind her. His heat enveloped her and overtook her senses. The roses became a distant memory, with his scent overtaking theirs. She had wanted nothing more than him. He lifted his hand and skimmed his fingers over her bare arms. "You're breathtaking," he said. His voice was hoarse as he spoke. "I am quite taken with you."

"Then it is good that I am with you as well." She closed her eyes and leaned into him. She wouldn't overthink this. Sometimes a lady had to let go and enjoy the moment. That was what Claudine needed more than anything. She always did the right thing. She wanted to be a different person, at least for a little while. One that took chances without a care for the future... She would do that with Hudson. "I have a proposition for you."

"Oh?" he said as he leaned down to trail kisses over her shoulder. "What do you have in mind?"

His kisses were like a heady drug. She had to

have this conversation before all talking became an impossibility. "One night." Her words came out breathy. "I'll spend one night with you. Then we go our separate ways and never speak of it again."

He stilled. Would he say no? She prayed he wouldn't, but she couldn't make assumptions. Just because he was interested, and a man, didn't mean he'd readily agree to this arrangement. She waited for him to answer. The anticipation was building inside of her and she didn't know if she could handle any more of this silence.

God help her... she wanted this man so damn much.

ONE NIGHT... THAT HAD BEEN WHAT HE WANTED, HADN'T it? Now that she was offering it to him, he didn't know what to say. Hudson did not want to say no, but he didn't like the limitations. He usually set the boundaries. How had it all been turned around on him? He found he didn't enjoy being on the other side of things. He had to handle this with care. If he wanted more than one night, then he'd have to agree to this plan of hers and find a loophole around it. What could he do to get her to agree?

He spun her around in his arms. His gaze met hers, and heat spread through him. She was so bloody beautiful. He reached behind her head and untied her mask. It fell off her face, and he caught it easily. "We won't be needing this, will we?"

She lifted a brow. "What about yours?"

Hudson grinned. "Do you want to remove mine?" He had no problem allowing her to do that. "Go ahead."

She lifted her hand and tugged on the ribbon, securing his mask in place. It came loose, and the mask slid down his face. She reached up and grabbed it, then tossed it to the side. "That's better. I enjoy seeing your entire face. The mystery is fun, but this is better."

"I couldn't agree more." He lifted her hand and pressed a kiss to her palm. "I would like one night with you." Hudson already decided he wanted more than that. Her stipulation had brought out a possessive side he hadn't expected. "I want to kiss you where ever I want." He demonstrated by pressing his lips to her wrist, then several more all the way down her arm. "I want to strip this decadent gown off of your body and kiss you as it slips from your gorgeous body." He leaned down and kissed her shoulder, then her neck. "I want to kiss you here."

He pressed his hand to the juncture between her thighs. "Until you're screaming with pleasure and you forget everything except the desire coursing through you." He slid his tongue over her neck lightly, then leaned so his mouth was near her ear. "Would you like that?"

"Yes." The word came out breathy. "All of it. Now."

He hadn't agreed to just one night. Hudson definitely didn't agree to never speaking of it again. He didn't make promises he couldn't keep. "Then let me show you how much pleasure I can give you."

"Here?" she said.

"Yes," he told her. "There's a large settee a little farther inside." He pulled her against him so her breasts were pressed against his chest. "On the other side where no one can look in and see us. Not unless they know where to look. Many of the plants will block their view."

"But someone could see." Her voice hitched a little. Did she like the idea of someone watching? That was interesting...

"If they're lucky," he began. "Yes..."

She nibbled on her bottom lip. "That's very naughty."

"It can be." He skimmed his hand over her hip. "Does that bother you?"

She shook her head. "Take me there."

Hudson didn't stop to question her decision. She wanted him, and he needed her. He led her to the settee at the back of the conservatory. He'd never been so grateful that the duke had installed it there. It also didn't do to question how many women Sinbrough had seduced in this conservatory. All that mattered was that he had Claudine all to himself. He would have her... finally. It hadn't been that long, but it felt as if he'd been waiting forever for her.

He turned her around and undid the buttons on the back of her gown. The bodice loosened enough that her breasts were bare. She had a thin, almost transparent chemise. He groaned at the sight. "So, so lovely." Hudson skimmed her bare skin with the back of his hand. He turned her around, then lowered his head so he could suck one of her perfect breasts into his mouth. She moaned when he sucked a rosy nipple, then turned his attention to her other breast.

"More," she demanded.

"All in good time," he told her. "We have the entire night."

"Yes..." She groaned as he sucked her nipple

again. He had to get the dress off. All of her clothing... He wanted her naked and writhing beneath him. Hudson made fast work of her entire outfit, then lifted her to set her on the settee.

"I'm going to taste every inch of you now." He didn't wait for her to reply. Hudson began doing exactly as he had told her. He kissed her belly, then her thighs. She shivered as he trailed his lips over her naked flesh, but when he settled between her thighs, she opened them willingly. She wanted him to make her scream with pleasure, and he couldn't wait to hear her moan.

Hudson licked her sex slowly and got the first quiet moan from her. Then he sucked the sensitive nub into his mouth and her hips bucked. He held her down and continued to tongue her. When her moans quickened, he knew she was close. He slid a finger into her, then sucked harder. She screamed his name as her climax overtook her. It was the best thing he'd ever heard.

As she lay languidly on the settee, he stripped all of his clothes off. When he was fully naked, he joined her there. "Are you ready for more?"

"I'm not sure if I can handle any more pleasure."

"You can," he reassured her. "And I intend to

prove that to you. There is no such thing as too much pleasure."

She closed her eyes and sighed. "Then do your worst, my lord."

"No," he said. "You'll have my best. Always."

He began to kiss her again until she was breathless with need. Then he settled between her thighs. He had to be inside her. This time they would find their pleasure together, and later he'd taste her again. Hudson fully intended to make this one night she wouldn't easily be able to walk away from.

Hudson slid inside of her. She groaned and wrapped, lifted her legs until her knees pressed against his hips. He began to slide in and out of her in slow, even strokes. She felt so bloody good. How could he have lived this long without feeling this before? There had never been anything like this... He lost all ability to think and whatever finesse he'd possessed before had been lost. His pace quickened, and there was no rhyme or reason to it.

This time, he moaned her name as he climaxed. What the hell had just happened? He'd been with many women before, but none had left him mindless. Claudine meant more... He just didn't quite understand what exactly that more was or what to do about it.

Ten

Claudine sat in the sitting room waiting for Eden to join her. Two days ago she'd had her one night with Hudson and still, she could not stop thinking about him. What made her believe that she could so easily forget about him? Especially after a night like that... He'd brought her pleasure over and over again until he'd exhausted them both. His kiss was permanently imprinted on her. She would never be able to forget him. Her mind was out of control with thoughts of him. When she closed her eyes, all she could see was him, and her body came to life, remembering his touch.

She would never be the same again. Her feelings

for him were far stronger than she could have imagined. Claudine had thought she loved James. That was why she'd agreed to marry him before he left England. They had both been so young. His father had bought that commission for him. It was a respectful career for the younger son of a viscount. They'd had so many ideas of what their future would look like.

None of that had come to pass. She remembered everything about her time with her husband. Everything all came back to him and her decision to marry. It was time to truly let it all go and move on. It was so damn hard to do that, though. She knew now that her love for him was full of innocence and hope. They were nearly children when they said their vows. They thought they had the entire world ahead of them. Now she knew the truth.

Nothing was ever guaranteed. Life had a way of destroying all the carefully laid plans a person could make. She would never touch or kiss James again. They would never lie together and discuss their future or the children they would have. He died. James had left her alone to discover her path on her own. He hadn't even done it in a way that she could respect, and she didn't mean his death in battle.

He'd left her in his father's care without discussing it with her. James had made decisions about what was best for her, as if she were a child incapable of doing it for herself. She could forgive him for making those assumptions, but she couldn't forget about it. If she did, she might never gain the control she desperately needed with her life.

She had so much love to give. There was only one man she wanted to give it to, but she was afraid to do it. What if he rejected her? She had asked for one night with him and he hadn't exactly agreed to her proposal, but that hadn't stopped him from seducing her thoroughly. They had some passion between them that was undeniable. That could be the beginnings of something special. If she was willing to take a chance with him... She wouldn't beg him to love her. She would never let a man have that much control over her ever again.

But with Hudson... Could she show him what she needed? Would she be able to share all her hopes and dreams along with the fears? When the sun rose on the day...he hadn't pushed her away. He'd made sweet love to her again. When she'd insisted on dressing and leaving, he hadn't begged her to stay. He'd walked with her back to the town-house and helped her into a carriage. He'd been quiet the entire time. She didn't know what that meant. At the time, she believed he'd been abiding by her terms, but was he as conflicted as her? Did he want more, too? Should she have asked?

Claudine had so many questions and no answers. She should write him a note and send it to his townhouse. What had Lady Wyndam said he'd named it? Lockley House... It wasn't far from Eden's London home. She could have it sent and he could pay a call on her. Eden wouldn't mind if she had a caller. But what would she say to him?

Before she could overthink it, she sat at a nearby writing desk and pulled out a piece of parchment. She wrote quickly, without stopping to consider anything. If she did, she might not actually send it. After it was written, she went to find a footman.

"Can you deliver this to Lord Wyndam and Lockley House." she asked the footman.

"Yes, Mrs. Grant," he said. He took the note then left her alone in the parlor. He'd have it soon, and then he would come to see her. She didn't know how long it would take. He might not even be at home. She nibbled on her bottom lip. Had she just made a grave error?

"What has you so pensive?" Eden asked. She was standing at the bottom of the stairs, staring at her.

"I made a decision and now I'm fretting over it," she confided.

Eden smiled. "You want more than one night, don't you?"

Claudine nodded. They hadn't discussed in detail what had happened that night. Eden had met someone too, but she didn't know his name. All she knew for certain was it hadn't been the Duke of Sinbrough. She hadn't wanted to be one of his many conquests. They had both set aside their pasts that night. "I might be in love with him."

"Might be?" Eden lifted a brow. "How can you be certain?"

"I don't know. I thought I understood what love was, but I have found I don't know a darned thing."

"Why don't we go for a walk in Hyde Park? It's not going to be as crowded this time of day and we should enjoy this wonderful weather we're having."

Claudine nodded. Hudson wasn't likely to stop by so soon. He wouldn't rush over to Moreland House and find her. She would have some time to enjoy a walk. It might help calm her, too. "What a wonderful idea. Let me grab my spencer and I'll meet you here."

She rushed to her room and then joined Eden in the parlor again. They left for Hyde Park. They walked in silence. It was one thing she liked about her friend. They didn't need to talk. It was enough that they kept each other company.

They reached the park and strolled along the path set aside for those walking. There were a few carriages and some men on horseback, but they didn't pay any of them any mind. They were lost in their own thoughts. It wasn't until someone shouted her name that she stopped and glanced around her. She didn't have many regrets, but at that moment, she wished she had stayed indoors. The Viscount of Artcrest was strolling toward her and he didn't look particularly happy to see her. Damn and blast...

HUDSON SAT IN HIS STUDY, UNABLE TO FOCUS ON anything. He'd been staring at some household ledgers for the better part of an hour. The numbers kept blurring before him and he would instead be thinking about Claudine. Surely she couldn't actually think that one night had been enough. Hudson feared he wouldn't be satisfied with anything but forever.

That couldn't be right, though. That would mean

that he wanted something he had declared he would never have. He didn't want a wife. He sure as hell didn't want a future that included children. That was a disaster in the making. His grandfather, and both of his parents, had died young. Only his grandmother had made it this far. What if he was destined to die young, too? What if he married Claudine and then she died in childbirth like his mother had?

Would he be like his father and leave his child on his own? Who would raise them if that happened? His grandmother was not young enough to handle that and with his parents gone... Hell, he didn't even know if Claudine's parents lived. Somehow, he doubted they did. If they had, why wouldn't she return to them now that she was a widow? There was something she hadn't told him, but he didn't know what it could be. He had to see her...

"Pardon the interruption," his butler said from the doorway. "But this just arrived for you."

"What is it?" Hudson frowned. Then he glanced at what the butler held. I was a missive of some sort. He really had to pay more attention. "You can set it on my desk. I'll look at it later."

He really should finish the accounting. It was important... The butler set the letter on his desk.

Instead of focusing on his ledgers, he stared at it. The handwriting seemed familiar. Like he'd seen it somewhere before, but he couldn't place it. He picked it up and broke the seal. When he read the words, he was on his feet instantly.

> Hudson,
> Please forgive my intrusion. One night...what was I thinking? Clearly I miscalculated. Will you pay a call on me? I'm visiting with the Dowager Countess of Moreland, but I'm uncertain how long I'll remain here.
> I await your reply.
> Claudine

He grinned. She wanted to be with him, too. He knew where to find her now. Now he had to discern the best way to approach her. She agreed one night wasn't enough, but what did that mean? Would she be interested in something far longer...like forever, or would she only agree to an affair with no time limits? He would accept anything, but he wouldn't accept she would not be a part of his life. As long as she wanted him, he had a chance of convincing her she belonged with him.

"What are you smiling about?" the Duke of Sinbrough asked. He strolled casually into his study and poured brandy into a glass. Hudson kept a decanter in his study for particularly trying days.

Hudson wasn't ready to tell him about Claudine. She was too important to gossip about. Instead, he decided to change the subject in favor of the duke. "How was your night with the lady in white?"

The duke frowned. "It didn't go as I would have liked." He swallowed the brandy. "She had no interest in me. Instead, she spent the evening with Carrington, the lucky bastard. I don't even know who she was."

Hudson tilted his head to the side. He suspected that the lady in white was the Countess of Moreland. She had arrived with Claudine, and according to her note, she was residing with the countess. Sinbrough had invited the young widow. He would be disappointed if he realized his near miss with her. "I am certain you found another woman to help heal your broken heart."

He snorted. "It wasn't that broken." The duke swallowed down the rest of his brandy. "How was your evening? Did your lady make you forget all your troubles?"

Hudson smiled. "My evening was far better than yours. I can guarantee it." He wiggled his eyebrows. "I didn't lose out to the Duke of Carrington."

Sinbrough narrowed his gaze. "That's rude, even for you. For that, I'm drinking more of your brandy."

"Help yourself. You always do." Hudson laughed. "But I'm not going to stay much longer. I have another appointment."

"With the lady from the other night?" Sinbrough asked as he poured more brandy. "Isn't it early in the day for an assignation?"

"It's never too early for the right woman," he said. Hudson didn't want to admit he was rushing over to see Claudine, though. "I am off to Wyndam House."

"Ah," the duke said. "You had me scared for a moment there. But visiting your grandmother makes sense. Especially this time of day... I suppose that is what you meant by the right woman." He drank more brandy. "She's the only one you deem important enough."

That had been true in the past. It wasn't the same now. He wanted Claudine to be by his side. Once she agreed to that, he would openly admit it to anyone that asked. Until then, he would keep his aspirations to himself. "Enjoy the brandy," he told the duke. "I'll see you later at the club." They had a game scheduled with a few close friends. He actually wasn't certain why the duke had come by. He'd ask him later. For now, he had something far more important to do.

Eleven

After her encounter with the viscount at Hyde Park, Claudine had left London immediately. She had run when he started toward her. It had been embarrassing to admit, but she feared if he had reached her she would now be residing at his country home. Before she had married James, she hadn't actually met his family. He had an older brother that was to inherit the title and a younger sister that would have a season soon. She would make her debut along with Eden's sister-in-law, Roslyn. She'd gone to see them when she received news of James' death.

It was then that the viscount had revealed James' intentions for her. She'd abided by them for as long as she could. After Lady Wyndam had approached her about joining the league, she'd packed her meager belongings and left the viscount and his rules behind. Surely he couldn't actually force her to remain there... He would try to, though. Claudine hated anything that would cause a scene. She preferred to stay in the shadows. That was why attending balls never truly appealed to her.

The masquerade had been an exception. No one paid her any mind. They were all there for one purpose, and no attendee wanted to let society know their identity that night. She'd felt comfortable going with Eden. Her one regret after crossing paths with the viscount was that she hadn't been able to visit with Hudson. She had left London suddenly. That had been six weeks earlier...

She had to return to London and not just because Lady Wyndam had sent a reminder about the upcoming council meeting. It was time to accept what her future would hold. She didn't want to admit it, but there was no choice, and she wouldn't regret any of the decisions she had made.

The carriage rolled across the cobbled path that led to Wyndam House. The countess was expecting her, of course. Her usual room would be prepared, and in a few days, they would have their normal meeting. She couldn't think of any of that, though.

There was only one thought on repeat in her mind. Hudson. She wished she could have seen him before she left London. Would he even wish to see her now? Had he tried to call on her before?

Eden was fully embroiled in the season now. She hadn't written once. She had to chaperone Roslyn. If Hudson had visited her townhouse, surely she would have written Claudine. That must mean he didn't think of her quite the same way as she did. Claudine wished she could walk away and not give him a second thought. She had a lot of truths to face. There were several big ones, including that she loved the man. There were no doubts there. She wouldn't have given herself to him fully if her heart hadn't been engaged. If only she had realized that fact sooner... There was no going back now and she didn't want to.

The carriage came to a stop, and not long after, the door opened. She expected a footman to be there to help her out, but it wasn't. Hudson stood there, staring at her. His gaze was filled with something, but she couldn't discern it. She was too shocked to see him to form proper words. He held out his hand to her, and she tentatively placed hers in his. He assisted her out of the carriage and they walked in silence into Wyndam House. What was he doing there?

"Hudson..."

"Not yet," he said. "Let's go inside."

She swallowed the lump in her throat. It was so lovely to gaze upon him. He seemed angry. Was that the emotion she saw in his gaze? She didn't understand any of this. Had Lady Wyndam known he would be there? Why hadn't she said anything in her missive? Hell, why would she have? As far as she was aware, the countess wasn't aware of what had transpired between Claudine and her grandson. What would she think of her if she discovered it all?

Her stomach rolled, and she barely held back the queasiness that had overtaken her. She wouldn't think about any of that. It wasn't important at this particular moment. She had to focus on Hudson and try to discern what was happening. They walked into the sitting room. No one was around. Where was the countess? She usually sat in the room for most of the day. Juliet shouldn't be far behind either.

Hudson folded his hands behind his back and rocked back on his heels. He stared at her expectantly. Almost as if he knew something she hadn't yet told him. How was that even possible? "I've been waiting for you."

She tilted her head to the side. "I gathered as much." What else was she supposed to say? She didn't know what he expected from her.

"I went to Moreland House," he told her. "The butler explained that you and the countess had gone for a walk. I went to Hyde Park to look for you."

He had? "I didn't stay long."

"I gathered as much when I found Lady Moreland alone." He studied her in silence for a few moments. "Viscount Artcrest was quite distressed."

She bet he had been... "Is that so?"

"I didn't realize your husband was his son." He gazed at her. "There is a lot I don't know about you. Speaking with him made me realize why you speak little about yourself." He stepped forward but didn't reach out for her. "He's a harsh man."

"He can be," she agreed. "I think he means well."

"But you don't wish to be under his tender care," Hudson said with a nod. "I may be able to help you gain your freedom from him."

Claudine frowned. What did he mean by that? She didn't want him to concern himself over any of this. "I don't believe there is a need for that."

"Isn't there?" He lifted a brow.

She frowned. What did he mean? Claudine had never been more confused. She hadn't been able to stop thinking of him. Her heart hurt at the idea of never seeing him again. She prayed it wouldn't come to that. But he seemed so cold right now.

HUDSON'S HEART HAD BROKEN A LITTLE BIT WHEN HE realized Claudine had fled Hyde Park. He feared he would never see her again. No one would tell him where to find her. It had taken him weeks to convince his grandmother that he needed to see her. He fully believed even then she wouldn't have helped him if Claudine wasn't supposed to return to London, anyway.

The shadows in his soul had darkened at the thought he might lose her. He would never recover if he lost her. He knew that immediately after she'd left. In that way, he was very much like his father. Hudson wouldn't survive if she ever died. A part of him would always be with her. He prayed he would be strong enough to live if they had children that needed him. Either way, he wouldn't let her go easily. He fully intended to fight for her, for their future.

"You'll have to enlighten me," she said in a cool tone. "Because I don't know what you're implying."

He sighed. He was handling this all wrong. She was all he thought about, and if he didn't rein in his fear, he'd lose her. "Aren't you tired of hiding? Of running?"

She closed her eyes and took a deep breath. "I am," she admitted. "I'm done with that, though."

Hope filled him with her words. Had she come to the same conclusion he had? "Are you going to stay in London?"

"That depends on you," she told him. Her gaze was focused on him.

"Is that so?" Hudson held back a smile. If it was up to him, then she wasn't going anywhere. He fully intended to keep her by his side for the rest of their lives. Which he hoped would be a very long time. "What do you need from me?" He'd give her anything...say anything, as long as she agreed to be his forever.

She took a deep breath. "Our one night together..." Claudine paused, as if considering her words.

"Was the best night of my life." He would not regret their night together. It had made him open to a future that included her. He might never have come to that conclusion without that one night with her in his arms.

Her lips titled upward. "It was memorable."

Hudson stepped closer. "We can have more nights like that one." He wanted the right to hold her every night and wake up with her beside him. There would be no separate bedrooms for them. Once they were married, they would be by each other's side as much as possible. He didn't want to control her, but he also didn't want to be away from her either.

"Can we?" Her tone held a hint of amusement. "What about societal expectations? What if the ton frowned upon us repeatedly sharing a bed?"

"I don't care what anyone thinks." He took one more step closer to her. "You're all that matters to me."

"What if I don't want more nights with you?" She lifted a brow.

He closed his eyes and held back any curses that he wanted to let out. She was pushing back, trying to understand his intentions. That didn't mean she didn't want him. She never would have sent that note if she had no desire to be with him. But did she love him? "If you never wish to see me again, I'll try to respect your wishes."

"Try?" She blinked several times. "You don't think you can stay away?"

He groaned. "Sweetheart, you're in my blood." Hudson placed his hand on his chest. "My heart beats for you." He moved his hand, so he cupped her cheek. "I want to give you everything you need, but I need you. I don't know how long I could go without at least seeing your beautiful face. I'm lost on you."

A tear fell down her cheek. He wiped it away with his thumb. "Don't cry, love." It was breaking his heart. What had made her react like this?

"You're right," she began. "The viscount is a problem."

That was her reply to his heartfelt confession. He frowned. "I do know how to solve that. I believe I already mentioned that."

She nodded. "And I am willing to listen." Claudine stepped closer to him. There wasn't much space separating them now. He could wrap his arms around her and crush her against him. "But there are a few things I need to say to you first."

"Such as?" He could control his need to hold her a little longer. He could...

"I love you," she said. He hadn't said those words exactly, but she seemed to have understood what he'd been saying. His heart skipped a beat to hear her say she love him.

"I love you so much," he told her. His voice was hoarse as he spoke.

Another tear fell down her cheek. "I realize that now." She took his hand and placed it against her stomach. "Also, you're going to be a father."

He froze at her words. They had spent the night together, but he hadn't considered that possibility. He was usually so careful when he bedded a woman, but he had taken no precautions with Claudine. He stared down at his hand, then he glanced back at her. "You're certain?"

"As certain as a woman can be," she told him, then took a deep breath. "I planned on visiting you while I was in London. I was surprised, but glad, to see you already here."

Hudson grinned and pulled her into his arms. "Then this makes the next part so much easier." He leaned forward so that his lips hovered over hers. "You're going to marry me."

She laughed. "Don't you think you should ask me?"

"No," he said. "That gives you the opportunity to say no. Let's skip all that and accept that we are meant to be together. Besides, once you marry me, the viscount loses all control over your life."

"That's your grand plan?" She sighed. "I should have realized. You do know it won't be that easy? He's supposed to approve of my future husband."

Hudson grinned. "Then it is good, I've already gained his permission."

She blinked several times. "That's..."

"Genius?" He didn't think that was the word she was searching for, but he couldn't help himself. "I thought so too."

Claudine shook her head. "I should be mad, but I am too happy to be right now." she wrapped her arms around his neck. "Kiss me now. I've waited long enough."

"Anything you want, love," he told her, and then did as she demanded. He pressed his lips to hers. Their kiss was slow, deep, and as passionate as the love that burned through them. He'd found the one woman meant for him. He still had fears about their future, but as long as he had her by his side, he believed he could face them. And soon they would have their first child, which only meant he would have to marry her quicker than he had originally planned. What a blessing...

Epilogue

Five years later...

Hudson stood on the balcony overlooking the garden at Lockley House. His wife was down by the roses again. She leaned down and smelled the blooms and smiled. His heart leapt at that smile. Her happiness enveloped him and filled him with that same joy. He would never tire of being with her. She made everything better in his life.

Their son sat down on a blanket nearby with his baby sister. Niall was four now, and little Katherine, named after his grandmother, had just turned one. He'd been so frightened each time she'd carried their children and breathed a sigh of relief each time she made it through childbirth. He was content with the children they had, but she wanted a large family.

He should go down and join them. Hudson wanted to pull her into his arms and kiss her senseless. They were all so content he hated to disturb them. It was a pleasure to just have them near. He gave Claudine all the space she needed. He didn't want to overwhelm her.

"My lord," the nanny said as she stepped on to the balcony. "Do you wish for me to take the children inside for their nap?"

He glanced at her, then back down at the garden. They really should go inside. "Yes," he told her. "Tell my wife I'll join her shortly."

The nanny nodded and descended the stairs to the garden. Hudson went back inside and retrieved a present he had made for Claudine. Then he went back outside and down to the garden. She sat on a bench near the roses, waiting for him.

"What do you have there?" She lifted a brow.

"It's a journal," he held out the leather-bound book to her. "For you to write your own guidebook." After their wedding, she had told him about the league his grandmother had created. He'd always known she helped others, but he hadn't realized to what extent. Claudine had only told him because she fully intended to remain involved. She believed all the widows needed her, and she had a lot to offer.

"Oh," she said, then held the book against her. "What a lovely idea."

He hadn't read the guidebook that already existed. It wasn't his place to intrude on the widows or their little league. He was just glad he could keep his own former widow safe, and he intended to love her for as long as fate allowed. "If you fill this one, I can always have another bound for you."

"I think one is enough." She smiled at him, then set the journal next to her. "Why don't you sit down next to me? It's been forever since you last kissed me."

"It's been less than an hour," he told her, humor filling his tone. Then tilted his head to the side thoughtfully. "You're right. That's far too long."

She laughed as he pulled her into his arms. He slanted his lips over hers and kissed her, as she'd demanded. Then he lifted her into his arms and settled her into his lap. He wanted her. Hudson always wanted her. When it came to his Claudine, his love, he hadn't stood a chance, and he would not change one thing. She was his, and he belonged to her in every way.

Thank you so much for taking the time to read my book.

Your opinion matters!

Please take a moment to review this book on your favorite review site and share your opinion with fellow readers.

www.authordawnbrower.com

Excerpt: To Bargain with a Rogue

WICKED WIDOWS' LEAGUE BOOK THREE

Continue to the next book in the Wicked Widows' League

Blurb

*A **widow** strikes a **bargain** with a **rogue** and gets much more than she expected!*

Alicia Radcliff, Countess of Hawthorne, spent a decade married to a man she didn't like, let alone love. Now that she's a wealthy widow and a suitable mourning period has passed, she's determined to pursue happiness, beginning with finding a lover on her terms.

Matthew Ashton, Earl of Slayton, is in desperate need of a miracle. His recent inheritance consisted of a title, holdings that require repairs, and piles of debt. If it weren't for the need to help his sister make her debut, he'd turn his back on it all. Instead, he's searching for an heiress to marry. Quickly.

Alicia is struck by Matthew's gentle care of his sister as well as his handsome ruggedness, so different than other lords. A dance with the earl confirms he is the one for her.

Intrigued by the lovely widow and her fortune, Matthew proposes only to be shocked when Alicia counters with an offer of her own. A night of passion convinces him that she's meant to be his. Can he persuade her to change their bargain to one of love?

Order here: https://books2read.com/u/mqEwz1

Prologue

~~~~~

Alicia Radcliff considered her reflection in the dressing table looking glass, pleased to not see dull black bombazine staring back at her. Thrilled, in fact.

It had been a year and a day since her husband of nearly ten years had died. More than enough time to mourn a man she hadn't liked, let alone loved.

The lavender silk was still respectful of her status as a widow but a welcome change from the unrelenting black she'd endured the past year.

Having married at the tender age of eight and ten, she had quickly learned what was expected of her as the Countess of Hawthorne. Remain silent unless spoken to. Do not share an opinion even if asked. Smile politely and act as if happy and grateful for all that your husband has provided.

Those lessons had been harsh at times. *Damn him.*

She drew a breath to ease the tension that filled her at the thought of Frederick. He was gone—after a drunken ride on his horse in the dark of night—and she was determined to step out of his shadow and claim a new life.

A life of her choosing.

This evening, she would attend a dinner with an interesting group of women, one of whom had introduced herself last week while Alicia was at her modiste's. Mrs. Claudine Grant had mentioned that the ladies were all widows and invited Alicia to meet them.

Alicia was reserving her opinion until she'd had a chance to learn more, but the concept was intriguing—fellow widows who promised to support and guide each other in every way possible.

While ready to step into her own, Alicia was still finding her confidence. She hadn't known who she was since she'd married so young. Her husband had preferred her time be spent with him or at home. She had no true friends. Acquaintances? Yes. But people she could trust? That remained to be seen.

Much of the past year had been spent in solitude with her son, Charlie. At four years of age, he was a bright light in her life.

She'd missed many experiences thanks to marrying young and her husband's overbearing nature. Her father hadn't been concerned about such things when he'd accepted Frederick's offer on her behalf.

Alicia shoved away her bitterness. It wouldn't serve her. She'd done her duty as required by her family and her husband, though Frederick had been disappointed that she'd only provided him with one child. He'd forgiven her because that child had been a son—the heir he'd so desperately wanted.

All of that was behind her, she reminded herself. She was determined to look toward the future. The time had come to start anew. She was ready to experience a few adventures.

Many things were on her list, including developing new relationships. Finding true friends was a priority, but she also wanted to experience physical affection, something sorely missing in her marriage.

That meant possibly taking a lover.

She pressed a hand to her middle as nerves danced at the thought.

"Is something amiss, my lady?" Sarah, her new

lady's maid, asked. "Do you not care for your coiffure?"

"It's lovely." She tilted her head in the mirror, appreciating the curls Sarah had created from her normally straight dark hair.

Frederick hadn't liked curls.

"You look wonderful, my lady."

Alicia turned to smile at her. "Thank you, Sarah."

Alicia had dismissed much of the staff, giving them all excellent references, soon after her husband's death. She wanted as few reminders of Frederick as possible.

She'd liked Sarah from the moment she'd met her. The maid was no innocent young miss and encouraged Alicia to try new things. She was pleased that Alicia had at last put away her mourning wardrobe and thrilled to assist with a new coiffure.

"Your cloak and gloves are here when you're ready to leave." Sarah gestured toward a nearby chair. "Will there be anything else?"

"No." Alicia checked the clock on her desk that stood along one wall. "I'm going to see to some correspondence since I'm ready early." She wasn't due at Lady Wyndham's townhome, where the widow gathering was to be held, for another hour.

"Enjoy the evening, my lady." Sarah gave her a bright smile then curtsied and took her leave.

Alicia moved toward her desk and sat in the chair to pull out a sheet of paper before removing the inkwell lid. If she were going to take a lover, she would be intentional about it. And very selective.

In the past year, she'd come to realize that writing down her thoughts allowed her to better consider difficult decisions, and she'd had to make many of those since Frederick's death.

This decision was one that she intended to be pleasurable.

With a smile, she dipped her pen into the ink and started to write.

Qualities of the perfect lover.

Kind. That was imperative. Arrogance was acceptable but never cruelty.

Respectful. He had to respect her, and she would do the same for him.

Clever. She wanted an intelligent man who could carry on a stimulating conversation. Alicia wanted more than just the physical aspects of having a lover.

Humor. He needed to be able to make her laugh. She'd had little to smile about since marrying or during her year of mourning.

Now on to the more physical aspects...

She considered for a long moment before dipping her pen once again.

Butterflies. The moment he, whoever he was, looked at her, she wanted to feel flutters of awareness in her middle.

Toe-curling kisses. When they kissed, she wanted to feel it all the way to her toes. Though she wasn't certain it was possible, the few romantic tales she'd read insisted it was.

Experienced. He needed to know a woman's body better than she did.

Boundaries. She wanted a lover, not another husband. That was non-negotiable. Relationships were out of the question.

She read over the list, pleased with what she had thus far. There was no hurry. She intended to take her time to find the right man.

But first, she would meet with the widows and see what they had to say. Perhaps some would become friends. She dearly hoped so. If they had advice to offer, even better.

She rose from her desk, collected her cloak and gloves, and descended the stairs. Something told her that her life was about to change and for the better —starting with this evening.

Order here: https://books2read.com/u/mqEwz1

Excerpt: A Lady Never Tells

LADY BE WICKED BOOK ONE

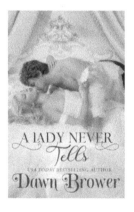

The first book in an all new series: Lady Be Wicked
featuring Eden, The Countess of Moreland from Her
Rogue for One Night

Blurb

Eden Barrett, the Countess of Moreland, is a young widow. Her foolish husband died in a duel, after having an affair with her closest friend. With one affair her entire life changed. Having freedom for the first time in her life she embraces it. Roslyn, her sister by marriage, is about to debut and Eden is her chaperone, and she's determined to aid her to find a husband that won't disappoint her.

Maxwell Holden, the Duke of Carrington has decided it is time to find himself a wife. He has a list of requirements and Lady Roslyn Barrett is the perfect candidate. There is only one problem: her chaperone. Something about her is oddly familiar, and he's more drawn to the young widow than he likes. The more time he spends with her, the more he can't stay away.

Eden is determined never to marry again. Especially to the Duke of Carrington. She has a secret though and if he discovers it everything will change. They've met before, and she's determined he never realizes exactly how they're acquainted. Secrets don't stay buried though, and this one is about to come to the light...

Order Here: **https://books2read.com/ALadyNeverTells**

Prologue

H er anxiety had hit an all-new level. Eden Barrett, the Countess of Moreland, did not take risks. It went against her very nature to do so. Yet, that was exactly what she was about to do. She'd willingly accepted an invitation to the Duke of Sinbrough's masquerade ball. It was literally entering into a den of iniquity. Sin itself would be on full display at this ball. The duke was famous for having the most debauched parties for anyone who wished to attend. It was rumored even the most strait-laced ladies would don a mask and join the festivities.

She should be all right. Shouldn't she?

If she kept telling herself that then perhaps, she would be. She'd convinced her good friend, Mrs.

Claudine Grant to attend the masquerade with her. She'd even commissioned scandalous costumes for them both. Eden's gown was the pure white of innocence, but it was anything but that. It was made for sin, and she hoped she would live up to the invitation it presented.

Her mask was also white to match the gown, but it had ruby red feathers fashioned to it on one side. A little splash of color to show she wasn't as innocent as the dress may suggest. Just in case the low-cut bodice didn't do the job. She had left her golden blonde hair loose and flowing down her shoulders. Her mask kept them from going wild, but if it was removed then they might just become unruly.

"Are you ready?" Claudine asked.

"As I'll ever be." She smiled at her. Eden tried to embrace her inner wickedness, but so far it seemed to be hidden. "Someone is about to approach us." She nodded slightly at the direction of two gentlemen making their way through the crowd. "I do believe the gowns are working." She'd had Claudine's gown designed in a decadent pink that nearly matched her friend's skin tone.

Claudine grinned. "One of them is the man I hoped to see tonight. I'd recognize him anywhere."

"How fortunate that he's noticed you as well."

When the two men reached their side Claudine's love interest stared at her briefly before he held out his hand and said, "Dance with me." Claudine went off with him willingly leaving Eden alone with the other gentleman.

"Would you like to take a spin around the floor." The man said.

There was definitely something sinful about him. His hair was as black as his clothing, and his eyes were a very pretty green. She tilted her head to the side and studied him. "You're the Duke of Sin aren't you."

"Was I being too obvious?" He grinned. "Would you like me to live up to that moniker?"

Eden wasn't interested at all in him. He might be sexy as well, sin, but she didn't find him all that interesting. She wanted to feel something. She didn't know exactly what, just that he didn't do anything for her. She shook her head. "No, thank you."

Someone laughed from behind her. "Have you lost your touch old man."

The Duke of Sinbrough frowned. "Don't be ridiculous. That would never happen." He wiggled his eyebrows at Eden as if that said everything. "We're just becoming acquainted."

Eden turned around to glance at the man who had just entered behind her. He didn't wear all black like most of the men in the room. However he had not bothered to wear a waistcoat and jacket. He had on dark blue pantaloons and a stark white shirt, but no cravat. He had left his shirt open giving her a nice view his neck, and part of his chest. The gentleman was completely disheveled. His hair wasn't nearly as dark as the Duke of Sinbrough's. It was more brown than black, but his eyes were a similar shade of green. Where she had found the duke's pretty, this man's were filled with heat.

That heat spread over her like a whirlwind. She'd been looking for someone to spark something in her. Eden had started to believe that she couldn't feel true passion. What was it about this man that made her want more? Was this desire? How had she never felt anything like it before. She took a step toward him and tilted her lips upward into what she hoped was a wanton smile. "Do you think you can do better?"

He returned her smile and it sent shivers right through her. "I know I can," he told her. "Would you like me to try?"

"You mean you haven't already?" She tilted her

head to the side. "Wasn't that what you were doing when you slid your way behind us?"

He chuckled softly. "You may be right." He leaned forward and said in a demanding tone. "I want you?"

"Do you?" She licked her lips. "I might let you have me." She stepped closer and trailed her finger over his collarbone. "But the night is still young. I have many options. What makes you my best choice?"

She'd never flirted like this in her entire life. Eden felt alive for the first time. The thrill of this was beyond even her wildest imagination. He stepped closer until her breasts rubbed against his warm chest. Her nipples tightened at the mere hit of his heat and the pleasure was intoxicating. He leaned down until his mouth was near her ear. His breath caressed her skin making her even hotter with need. "Darling," he said in a husky tone. "You already decided. Don't make me beg."

Her throaty chuckle sounded foreign to her ears. Who was this wicked, wanton, widow allowing this unknown gentleman to seduce her? She didn't recognize herself but wasn't that why she'd come to this masquerade. She slid her hand down and pulled out his shirt from his pantaloons, then slid it underneath until her fingers met his naked flesh. She trailed her fingers up his chest and then around his waist. He yanked her closer. "You're playing with fire, love."

"But what a burn it'll be," she replied in a husky tone. "You did say you wish to play with me tonight. Dazzle me with your skills."

"It'll be my pleasure," he said as he lowered his mouth. When his lips touched hers, she forgot everything, even her own name. Yes. This is what she had come to the masquerade for. She hadn't known what she'd been looking for until he'd come near. Damn this was good, and she suspected as the night rolled on she'd experience more passion than she'd ever known in her marriage.

She wanted him, and she'd have him. Then after this night she would go back to the proper Countess of Moreland. She had to keep up appearances after all. There were people that depended on her. But for this one night she could have him and all the pleasure this kiss promised. No one else had to know. A lady never tells her secrets, and this one she would always hold dear.

Order Here: **https://books2read.com/ ALadyNeverTells**

Wicked Widows' Books

RELEASE SCHEDULE AND ORDER LINKS

1. August 2022 **Dawn Brower—Wicked Widows' League**
2. March 21, 2023 **Dawn Brower—Her Rogue for One Night**
3. March 28, 2023 **Lana Williams—To Bargain with a Rogue**
4. April 4, 2023 **Cara Maxwell—Rogue Awakening**
5. April 11, 2023 **Ari Thatcher—My Lady Rake**
6. April 18, 2023 **Diana Bold—A Scoundrel in Gentleman's Clothing**
7. April 25, 2023 **Amanda Mariel—Rogue for the Taking**

8. May 2, 2023 **Courtney McCaskill —Scoundrel for Sale**

9. May 9, 2023 **Charlie Lane —Scandalizing the Scoundrel**

10. May 16, 2023 **Sue London—To Woo a Rake**

11. May 23, 2023 **Anna St. Claire—A Widow's Perfect Rogue**

12. May 30, 2023 **Rachel Ann Smith —Stealing a Scoundrel's Heart**

13. June 6, 2023 **Tracy Sumner—Kiss the Rake Hello**

14. June 13, 2023 **Nadine Millard —Seducing the Scoundrel**

15. June 20, 2023 **Jane Charles—Season of the Rake**

16. June 27, 2023 **Tabetha Waite—How to Choose the Perfect Scoundrel**

17. July 4, 2023 **Cecilia Rene—A Scandal with a Scoundrel**

18. July 11, 2023 **Shannon Gilmore—Kiss Me Like a Rogue**

Acknowledgments

Special thanks to Elizabeth Evans. Your encouragement and assistance with this book helped me immensely. I am grateful for all you do for me.

About Dawn Brower

USA TODAY Bestselling author, DAWN BROWER writes both historical and contemporary romance. There are always stories inside her head; she just never thought she could make them come to life. That creativity has finally found an outlet.

Growing up, she was the only girl out of six children. She raised two boys as a single mother; there is never a dull moment in her life. Reading books is her favorite hobby, and she loves all genres.

www.authordawnbrower.com
TikTok: @1DawnBrower

BB bookbub.com/authors/dawn-brower
f facebook.com/1DawnBrower
y twitter.com/1DawnBrower
o instagram.com/1DawnBrower
g goodreads.com/dawnbrower

Also by Dawn Brower

Always My Viscount

Infinitely My Marquess

Eternally My Duke

Bluestockings Defying Rogues

When An Earl Turns Wicked

A Lady Hoyden's Secret

One Wicked Kiss

Earl In Trouble

All the Ladies Love Coventry

One Less Scandalous Earl

Confessions of a Hellion

The Vixen in Red

Lady Pear's Duke

Scandal Meets Love

Love Only Me (Amanda Mariel)

Find Me Love (Dawn Brower)

If It's Love (Amanda Mariel)

Odds of Love (Dawn Brower)

Believe In Love (Amanda Mariel)

Chance of Love (Dawn Brower)

Love and Holly (Amanda Mariel)

Love and Mistletoe (Dawn Brower

The Neverhartts

Never Defy a Vixen

Never Disregard a Wallflower

Never Dare a Hellion

Never Deceive a Bluestocking

Never Disrespect a Governess

Never Desire a Duke

CONTEMPORARY

Stand alone:

Deadly Benevolence

Snowflake Kisses

Kindred Lies

Sparkle City

Diamonds Don't Cry

Hooking a Firefly

Novak Springs

Cowgirl Fever

Dirty Proof

Unbridled Pursuit

Sensual Games

Christmas Temptation

Daring Love

Passion and Lies

Desire and Jealousy

Seduction and Betrayal

Begin Again

There You'll Be

Better as a Memory

Won't Let Go

Heart's Intent

One Heart to Give

Unveiled Hearts

Heart of the Moment

Kiss My Heart Goodbye

Heart in Waiting

Heart Lessons

A Heart Redeemed

Kismet Bay

Once Upon a Christmas

New Year Revelation

All Things Valentine

Luck At First Sight

Endless Summer Days

A Witch's Charm

All Out of Gratitude

Christmas Ever After

YOUNG ADULT FANTASY

Broken Curses

The Enchanted Princess

The Bespelled Knight

The Magical Hunt

Ingram Content Group UK Ltd.
Milton Keynes UK
UKHW010646260323
419175UK00001B/6

9 798215 937877